Slocum turned his attention to the next lowlife, who hadn't made much progress in getting the girl to the alley. The man growled and grunted, all the while trying to rip her purse from her arms.

With a quick, short jab to the head, Slocum dizzied the lad enough that he lessened his grip on the girl's face. Then Slocum set himself up for another punch, this time to the man's now exposed midsection. Just before he landed it, the kid yowled a blue streak and lurched forward into Slocum's fist. It caught the kid square in the chest and he spun sideways, and kept spinning as if he were a schoolkid trying to dizzy himself up.

Soon enough he righted himself and took off lurching down the street.

Slocum dropped to a knee and extended his hands to help the girl. "Miss, you okay? Did they hurt—"

But that was all he was able to say because he felt a hot stab of pain in his left side, just below the ribs. "What did you do?" He pulled away his fingers and saw, in the scant light shed from the saloon windows, that his fingertips glistened. "You stabbed me." He looked at her. "You stabbed me!"

"I . . . I thought you were one of them."

He straightened up as she approached him, stiffening and turning his good side toward her. "You better think twice before you cut me again. Woman or no, I'll lay you out cold."

JAKE LOGAN

SLOCUM AND THE HIGH-COUNTRY MANHUNT

JOVE BOOKS, NEW YORK

THE BERKLEY PUBLISHING GROUP
Published by the Penguin Group
Penguin Group (USA) Inc.
375 Hudson Street, New York, New York 10014, USA

USA I Canada I UK I Ireland I Australia I New Zealand I India I South Africa I China

Penguin Books Ltd., Registered Offices: 80 Strand, London WC2R 0RL, England
For more information about the Penguin Group, visit penguin.com.

SLOCUM AND THE HIGH-COUNTRY MANHUNT

A Jove Book / published by arrangement with the author

Jove Books are published by The Berkley Publishing Group.
JOVE® is a registered trademark of Penguin Group (USA) Inc.
The "J" design is a trademark of Penguin Group (USA) Inc.

For information, address: The Berkley Publishing Group,
a division of Penguin Group (USA) Inc.,
375 Hudson Street, New York, New York 10014.

ISBN: 978-0-515-15381-1

PUBLISHING HISTORY
Jove mass-market edition / July 2013

PRINTED IN THE UNITED STATES OF AMERICA

10 9 8 7 6 5 4 3 2

Cover illustration by Sergio Giovine.

ALWAYS LEARNING　　　　　　　　　　　　　　　　　　　　**PEARSON**

1

Bismarck, North Dakota, hadn't been the place John Slocum intended to find himself, nearly broke, in the middle of winter. But when the last drive had ended back in Abilene, he'd agreed to work as an outrider for a freighting company. He'd done that for a number of months, right on through late fall, Christmas, and into the new year. And then, without warning, the company went belly up, leaving him stranded in Bismarck with his horse, his gear, and very few dollars in his pocket.

He also held a promissory note for his previous month's wages, which were to have been paid to him on his return to Abilene. But there was fat chance of ever seeing that cash. He'd had it on good authority that a long series of shady moves by the company's trusted accountant had wiped out the outfit's coffers.

When they heard the news, some of the teamsters had been quick enough to mosey to unknown areas farther west. These hired drivers figured it was their right to abscond with their mules, wagons, and loads in lieu of payment. Slocum couldn't blame them, but as an outrider, he had no such option. Best he figured he could do was hunker down in Bismarck for a spell, see if he could maybe deal some faro, or work for his and his horse's keep at the livery.

And that was just what he had done, biding his time, making enough to keep him and the horse in modest style with the occasional shot of bourbon and bate of oats to bolster their spirits. And they'd needed it a few times during a run of particularly dark, stormy days when it seemed nothing much happened except snow falling.

He didn't dare ride on out given the weather of late, but he figured that in another few days it would be February, and an old-timer at the bar swore his rheumatics told him they were in for a nice, long stretch of temperatures almost above freezing. That was good enough for Slocum. Anywhere south of Bismarck was a good direction—couldn't be worse.

On one mid-February day, the afternoon train churned into town, in the midst of this whited-out wash of grim winter landscape, where everyone did their best to stay drunk and not fight, and often succeeded too well at one and not well at all at the other. Normally the train hauled in very few interesting people, and goods most folks couldn't have afforded even if they'd wanted them. But on this particular frigid day, into the bar where Slocum and too many other men were drinking walked a singular young woman the likes of whom had rarely been seen in Bismarck.

She was bedecked from head to toe in what must have been high fashion. An ostrich-feather hat trimmed in rich black fur perched atop her high-piled honey blond hair. The hat bore deep purple accents that matched a long, glimmering purple satin dress that fit her fetching form so closely above the waist that she looked as if she'd been dipped in an artist's paint pot.

But it was her face that caught Slocum's breath in his throat. For a moment it even stopped his glass's motion in midair as it rose to his mouth.

She had such an unblemished complexion and a small pretty mouth, the corners of which seemed to hold an arched pose, as if in mischievous collusion with her clear green eyes, which seemed to take in everything all at once. Slocum decided she was both confident and as nervous looking as an abandoned fawn.

As a rule, Slocum was not all that interested in women who sported a fair amount of jewelry. But the adornments this woman wore reflected obvious wealth. Earrings that had the weight, luster, and glittering dignity of real gems matched her dazzling diamond choker. On most other women, Slocum thought that this combination of jewels, dress, hat, and long black gloves trimmed high with fur would look garish, might even hint at a dove trying too hard to impress. But on this young woman, whose bearing was so dignified, the effect was regal—and out of place. One look at her, and all activity in the vast barroom ceased.

A few seconds later, men unconsciously smoothed their hair, mustaches, and beards. They wiped their mouths to dislodge crusted tobacco residue that had built up after hours of fervent chewing, spitting, and gambling.

Slocum found he was as curious about her as every other soul in the Hoyt House Hotel and Bar. Curious enough that he kept an eye on her as she advanced across the room. All the while he felt pleased that he had chosen to do his afternoon's drinking here instead of the Crowhop Saloon—his usual spot, though only because the drinks at the Crowhop were taller and cheaper.

Instead of working to dispel attention and blend in—not much of a possibility in that crowd—Slocum was surprised to see the young woman stride up to the largest games table, at the back of the place, the spot reserved for serious gambling.

"Gentlemen," she said, placing her gloved hands on the back of the table's one empty chair. "Might I sit in on a hand or two?" Her voice was like a tinkling bell. Without waiting for an answer, she slid the chair out from the table and sat down.

In such an instance, it could have been all too common and easy to laugh in the pretty young thing's face. But there was something about her that seemed like she would not tolerate such boorish antics. Something about her told them all that regardless of her motives for joining them, here was a lady, a delicate but bold creature in their midst, something as uncommon in Bismarck in winter as a slender rose blooming in a snowdrift.

Once they got over their shock at this unexpected and odd development, several men at the table, and a few from nearby, jumped to their feet—too late—to help the young woman with her chair.

Who says manners don't stick with a man, even after years away from his mama? Slocum smiled and turned back to his drink, keeping an eye on the purple-clad beauty and curious about her boldness. He was eager to see what sort of a gambler she would turn out to be.

He didn't have long to wait. One of the men at the table began to dole out the cards. Slocum sipped his drink and noted that all at the table looked bright-eyed and uncomfortable. The girl, on the other hand, seemed most amused and looked to be having a fine old time.

Slocum assumed she must be staying at the Hoyt House, the fanciest accommodation in town, since she had strolled into the bar without any outerwear or luggage. He bet she was staying in one of the fancy rooms on the third floor, none of which saw frequent visitors.

He shifted his attention back to the game. Before long it became painfully obvious that the woman, as commanding a presence as she had, sported just the opposite in the way of card games. It was outright embarrassing, in fact. She'd set her purse, a small purple thing trimmed in fur, atop the table beside her. As the game progressed, she dipped into it with more frequency, recklessly pulling out a wad of paper money and high-denomination coins that shone in the smoky light of the bar. Here was a wealthy young woman and, noted Slocum, one whose initial confidence and boldness were on the wane.

As always happened in such situations, the men in the place acted as wolves closing in on a helpless fawn. They all but slavered every time the foolish young thing opened her purse. Greed glinted in their eyes, and soon Slocum saw them scrutinizing her glittering pretty things, the jewels that adorned her neck and ears and one wrist.

What was she thinking? What was her game? A conniving woman out to dupe the locals by first seducing them with false innocence? Somehow he didn't think so. She looked genuinely innocent and genuinely scared.

Slocum nursed the rest of his beer and watched, as most everyone else in the place did now, with unvarnished interest. One curious thing he noticed about the young woman was that she seemed to spend a lot of time watching the faces of not only her tablemates but those in the crowd around her. This was not the demeanor of a person serious about her card game.

It meant one of two things: She was woefully inexperienced at gambling, or she was looking for someone. Either way, she was playing poorly and losing money at a rapid rate. It was her business, of course, but it was foolish to Slocum nonetheless.

With his back to the bar, he took the opportunity to scan the crowd. Situations like this always brought out the seediest creatures looking for an easy slide of it. And before too long he spied one—a tall, thin goober whose ratty face wore frostbite like some sport two-day beards. He appeared to have trouble with one eye, and every so often his head twitched once, then twice, as if engaged in little nods. But he was directing his sight line across the crowd toward . . . who?

And then Slocum saw him, a thicker, shorter blond man, unkempt and with a moth-eaten wool cap riding high on his unwashed hair. He, too, appeared to be experiencing the same facial tics that afflicted the tall, rat-faced man. Slocum sighed. Surely it wasn't a coincidence. Even as he thought it, the second man nodded to the first, who appeared to melt back into the crowd and make his way to the door, then he slipped outside. No one noticed. No one but Slocum.

As he scanned the rest of the room, and kept an eye on the blond man, Slocum knew them to be common dry gulchers, thieves of the lowest order just waiting for their chance to prey on the young, foolish woman. He wondered how long she might hold out at the table. Her wad of cash had diminished somewhat, having made its way from her purse to the center of the table, but she still had plenty to offer, assuming her jewelry was as valuable as it appeared to be.

It didn't take the earlier mood of the men at the table long to turn from cautious, curious, and mildly bemused to smug, loud, and too confident. And Slocum noted that the same thing happened in reverse with the young woman. Despite all her seeming confidence when she had approached the table, she had no business sitting in with those men, none of whom appeared to him to be a professional gambler, but all of whom appeared to be able to hold their own at most any games table throughout the West.

The girl? If she was lucky, her skills might best be suited to a friendly game of whist at home in a parlor back East somewhere, with an elderly aunt or a kid brother. But not here in the frozen, bitter North, where men killed other men over the outcome of a card game—or the direction one might be headed.

Slocum swigged his beer again, polished it off, and as he wiped the back of his hand across his mouth, he reckoned the girl had about reached the end of her tether. For the first time he saw cracks appearing in her cool and collected façade.

Even from his distance, back to the bar, Slocum saw her mouth tighten into an unflattering rigid line, and her chin tremble ever so slightly.

Fold, he willed her with his mind. Fold and get the hell out of that game, girl. Get out before they eat you alive and leave you with an empty purse, no jewelry, and a sore hand from writing out IOUs.

And wonder of wonders—she laid down her remaining cards, smiled demurely, and held up her hands, palms out, in the universal sign of backing off. The hue and cry rose as the men around the table all whined, their greedy lips pooched out, their cigars nubbing down to little stubs from their fervent suckling. But she would not be dissuaded, and Slocum breathed a little sigh of relief for her.

Then he remembered the grungy blond man. Try as he might, he could not locate him again in the crowd. Had he, too, slipped outside? What were they planning? And then it occurred to him: This was one of those establishments that, while it shared a kitchen with the first-floor dining room of the hotel, made its patrons enter and exit through a side street front door.

Any guests of the hotel also had to enter and leave the saloon via the side street door. Slocum guessed it was that way because so few patrons of such a fine hotel spent as much time in the saloon as the locals, and the hotel owner probably didn't want locals tramping through the lobby instead of outdoors after a night of drinking. Understandable, but inconvenient for the rare gambling hotel guest.

All that mattered was the tight ringing feeling he got in the back of his head, the chiming sound in his skull that warned him danger was afoot. The girl had gathered her purse and nodded to her fellow players. But now that they had a wad of her money, few of them fawned as they had when she'd first showed up. Only one old soak offered to pull out her chair for her. The rest, Slocum shook his head over. He was good and sick of this town, and the winter was only half over. As he kept promising himself, the first chance he got, he was heading south.

He admired the woman as she walked to the door, and he moved in that direction himself. No one seemed to pay her much mind now that the commotion at the table had bubbled to a frenzied level of excitement.

As he strode by the table, Slocum overheard a flurry of voices, snatches of excitement: "See them diamonds?" "How much more you figger she's got?"

As much as he wanted to keep out of other people's affairs, and had done his best to remain quiet and unhindered in Bismarck, this girl would bear watching and might well be in trouble before her stay was over. He decided to follow her, even though he knew he'd be courting danger should he poke his nose in where it didn't concern him. Mostly because he himself was a wanted man, wanted wrongfully for a murder back in his home state of Georgia—not that his innocence had ever mattered.

As he headed to the door, he flipped up his coat's sheepskin collar. He hoped like hell the warning feeling he was getting about those two characters was wrong, though so far it hadn't ever let him down. Always a first time, he thought as he stepped outside and into a frigid blast of raw winter air. But a short, clipped scream from below on the boardwalk told him he'd not been wrong. The girl was in trouble.

2

The darkness of early evening, coupled with the heavy snows and gusting winds, made visibility difficult on the street. But not bad enough that he couldn't see the shapes of three people tussling, two of them larger than the third, and trying to drag the third down past the saloon to the waiting shadows of the alley.

Slocum pivoted on one hand, vaulting over the railing, landing him but a few feet from the scuffling throng. The girl wasn't screaming anymore, so she must have had her mouth covered. He hoped they hadn't knifed her into silence. One more stride and he managed to grab a handful of each of the men's coats. The smaller, Blondie, managed to twist out of his grasp. His coat had been thicker, a woolen mackinaw, more difficult to maintain a grasp on. The taller of the two, Rat Face, lost his grip on the girl and spun on this unseen attacker. Slocum landed one hard punch to the side of his head. The beanpole went down like a breeze-blown house of cards and lay still. He emitted nothing but an involuntary grunt as he hit the frozen ground, his head bouncing in a teeth-chattering rhythm.

Slocum turned his attention to the next lowlife, who hadn't made much progress in getting the girl to the alley. He still had her mouth covered with a grimy hand, but Slocum saw her legs lashing out, the white of her petticoats flouncing as she kicked and thrashed. She appeared to be more wildcat than he'd suspected she'd be.

The man growled and grunted, not making any real words, but all the while trying to rip her purse from her arms. She had it hugged tightly to her belly with both arms.

Slocum finally managed to discern who was who and he grabbed for the man's coat collar again and snagged a handful of wool. This time he stayed with it, and dragged on the man. But Blondie still wasn't letting go of the girl.

With a quick, short jab to the head, Slocum dizzied the lad enough that he lessened his grip on the girl's face. She took full advantage of the newfound freedom, not to scream as he'd expected, but to keep on lashing and thrashing. She must have bit down on the man's hand because he hissed as if he'd been stung.

Slocum set himself up for another punch, this time to the man's now exposed midsection. Just before he landed it, the kid yowled a blue streak and lurched forward into Slocum's fist. It caught the kid square in the chest and he spun sideways, and kept spinning as if he were a schoolkid trying to dizzy himself up.

Soon enough he righted himself and took off lurching down the street. Slocum wanted to go after him, but the girl had fallen backward when Blondie spun away from her.

Slocum dropped to a knee and extended his hands to help her. "Miss, you okay? Did they hurt—"

But that was all he was able to say because he felt a hot stab of pain in his left side, just below the ribs. Had he been shot? He didn't think that rat-faced man had enough gumption to shoot, not if he'd had the chance to vamoose.

No, he hadn't heard any sounds, and as he slumped backward to sit on his haunches, he saw no one on the boardwalk above. In fact, not a soul in the saloon had heard a thing, so quiet had the scuffle been.

"Hey, ma'am, are you okay?"

Slocum held his side and advanced toward her on his knees. But she, also on her knees, retreated from him, straight into a drift, although she didn't seem to care. She scrambled to her feet, kept backing from him.

"Ma'am, did they hurt you?"

"Stand back!" she said in a voice low and controlled. Though she was barely visible in front of the saloon, Slocum saw that she held her arm out in front of her, waving it back and forth as though it were a snake defending itself. "I'm not afraid to give you another one."

"What? Another what? Ma'am, I was just trying to help you get away from those thieves." What had she said . . . give him another one? "Ma'am, what did you do?"

She must have believed him, at least a little bit, because she stopped waving her arm, but still held it poised, as if ready to strike.

"What did you do?" He pulled away his fingers and saw, in the scant light shed from the saloon windows, that his fingertips glistened. "You stabbed me." He looked at her. "You stabbed me!"

"I . . . I thought you were one of them. Oh! Look out!" She pointed toward him. He turned in time to see the lanky form of Rat Face hobble down the street. Slocum's instinct told him to take off after the varmint, but the stitch in his side, from whatever it was she did to him, hurt like hell.

He took one, two strides, then gripped his side. "Damn, girl. I can't believe you stabbed me." He straightened up as she approached him, stiffening and turning his good side toward her. "You better think twice before you cut me again. Woman or no, I'll lay you out cold."

"Oh, stop your silliness." She held up her hand and he flinched, then looked closer. Something glinted, something long and thin. "It was only my hat pin." Then he noticed that her fancy hat was indeed lopsided and a handful of loose curls had escaped and framed one side of her face. Despite the hot little pain in his side, he had to admit the look was a good one on her.

"You ever been stabbed by a hat pin, ma'am?"

"Well . . . no."

"When you do, then you can tell me to stop my silliness. Until then, I'll bleed and I'll complain about it, thank you very much." He straightened and kept his right hand on the tiny wound. Hat pin or no, it hurt like hell. He hoped it hadn't punctured anything vital inside. He expected he'd have to go to the doc now, see what he might tell him, signs to look for just in case something inside was leaking.

"Now, for the last time, did they hurt you, ma'am?"

She shook her head, but was silent.

"And they didn't take anything?"

"No, I believe I have it all, my purse, my jewels."

"Good, then I suggest we report it to the marshal. This sort of thing can't stand—"

"No! No, thank you. I don't want the law involved. No harm done . . . well, except to you. But no, no law, please."

Despite being curious about her absolute determination that this go unreported to the law, Slocum had to admit he felt relief. As a longtime wanted man himself, he hadn't liked the idea of going voluntarily into a lawdog's office to report a crime, have his name taken down. He doubted the man would have a dodger on him, given the distance from Georgia to North Dakota, and the years that had passed, but in a town of this size, you never could tell who knew what.

As soon as she said it, she looked down toward her feet. He saw that the shock of the scuffle must have been wearing off because her shoulders rose up and down slightly. Crying. Great, he thought. Not only did I *not* get the lowlifes, but I'm stuck with a crying young woman who stabbed me.

He reached out a hand, touched her sleeve. "Hey, it's okay. They're gone."

To his surprise, she didn't pull away or flinch, just stood and sobbed quietly, as if she'd found out that her dog had died. "Let's get you inside, ma'am. It's too cold out here for that shawl you're wearing." He held out an arm and she took it. He turned back toward the buildings behind them. "I assume you're staying in the Hoyt House?"

She nodded, sniffed, touched her face with a hanky.

"Well, let's get you in there before you catch pneumonia." He guided her to the steps and tried to ignore the stinging in his side where the hat pin had punctured him. They made it to the warm lobby, where the girl detached herself from him and hustled over to the clerk's desk, behind which a portly man in a vest too small for him looked up from a newspaper.

His eyes immediately brightened and his smile was wider than Slocum thought possible on a human.

"Why, Miss Garfield!" As the clerk spoke, his hands, like two shaved pink rats, hurriedly folded the newspaper and stuffed it under the counter. His eyes never left her face. "I do hope you enjoyed yourself at our gaming tables."

Slocum figured she was going to retrieve her key and head on up to the confines of her room to sleep away the bad experiences she'd had in town. Somehow he didn't figure her for one to be so rude as to not even offer a smile and a nod to him, not that he was looking for thanks. But she did stab him, after all. He turned to head on out, had his hand on the cut-glass knob, when her voice said, "Hold on there, don't go just yet . . ."

He kept his hand on the knob, but looked her way. "Me?"

"Yes, you. I . . ." She held up a single finger in the air, telling him to wait, and turned back to the smiling desk clerk. "My dear old friend"—she nodded quickly toward Slocum—"and I would like to have supper in my rooms."

"But ma'am, I believe the kitchens are closed—"

"As I was saying . . ." She unclasped her purse. "We will require a complete meal, delivered to my rooms." She eyed Slocum, as if sizing him up for something, then said, "Two steak dinners, I think, yes, that will work, and dessert—cook's choice. And champagne, wine, and port." She looked at Slocum again. "And a bottle of your best bourbon. And an assortment of cigars, I think. Yes, cigars. Also, we will require medical supplies—bandages, medicinal alcohol, that sort of thing."

The clerk, red-faced, had snatched up a pencil and begun scratching down the list halfway through her recital.

She waited for him to finish, watching what he wrote, then nodded.

"Will that be all, Miss Garfield?"

"For now. Thank you. And if you could send up the champagne, the bourbon, and the medical supplies right away, it would be appreciated." Her smile had the same effect on the clerk as it did on Slocum—and neither man could help it. Even in a lopsided hat, she could melt ice at the North Pole.

She walked back to Slocum, who hadn't moved from the doorway, and held out her arm as he had to her not long before in the snowy street. "Shall we?" she said, smiling that smile and nodding toward the grand staircase.

He nodded. "Apparently we shall," he replied, and they walked up the stairs.

Neither of them spoke as they ascended the stairs, and after the first flight, Slocum felt the stitch in his side ease a bit. He reckoned—hoped—that her hat pin hadn't done as much damage as he'd initially suspected. He wanted to pull his hand out from inside his coat to see how bloody the thing had gotten, but he figured he'd wait until they got to her room. Or rooms, as she'd said. How big were her "rooms" anyway?

As he had guessed, those rooms were on the top floor of the Hoyt House Hotel. In fact, up in that rarified place, it appeared that they took up half of the upstairs. Slocum found himself both relieved that they had made it to the top floor and momentarily stunned at the enormity of what appeared to be just her sitting room.

"Please, come in."

He did, slipping off his hat and running a hand through his hair. He breathed a sigh of relief at having, just that afternoon, bathed, shaved, and pulled on fresh duds. The downside was that her hat pin trick had probably ruined his best shirt.

She closed the door behind him, then crossed the room, pulling off her fancy hat—which he didn't fail to note was secured by two more pins of surprising length. He gulped once.

"Ma'am—"

"Ginny. Please call me Ginny." She disappeared into an adjoining room and came back out, without her hat and holding an earring. "Please do forgive me, sir." She advanced on him, her hand held out.

He resisted the urge to back up, unsure if she was about to jab him again. She only wanted to shake hands.

"You saved me from some grim fate and I am afraid I don't even know your name."

The look of genuine concern on her face made him smile. "Slocum. John Slocum. Glad to be of service." He nodded, but she held on to his hand, looked at it.

"Oh my stars, I . . . I did that to you, didn't I?"

He looked down at his hand, too, and saw that it was stained with partially dried blood. Some had gotten on her hand.

She pulled open his coat and gasped. "I knew we'd need to doctor you, but I . . ."

Before she could finish giving voice to her thought, she brought a hand to her forehead and crumpled into him, her knees buckling.

Slocum tossed his hat aside and just managed to catch her. "Ma'am? Miss Garfield?" He held her draped in one arm, and lightly slapped her cheeks with the other. "Ma'am?"

No response. "Out cold," he said and scooped her up. He walked to the door she'd gone into before and saw a massive poster bed with a canopy of some gauzy blue fabric. The rest of the room's furnishings were ornate, with gold-painted accents, and little cupids seemed to adorn every corner and angle.

"Good Lord," he said as he laid her on the bed and stretched her legs out, smoothed her hair and dress.

He looked at her a moment, admiring her boldness and beauty, all in one fancy-wrapped package. He shook his head and left the room. All he really wanted to do was leave her be, let her sleep off her little fainting spell. He bent to retrieve his hat from the floor. As he punched a dent out of the crown, someone knocked on the door. "Room service, Miss Garfield."

"Oh hell," said Slocum. So much for vamoosing without any fuss. He sighed and opened the door.

The fat little red-faced desk clerk stood before him, holding a silver tray on which stood a bottle of champagne in a silver ice bucket. A towel was draped over it, and beside it stood a bottle of bourbon, a couple of glasses specific to their purpose, and an assortment of tinctures, bandages, and pins, plus scissors and other sundries.

"Where would you like this, sir?"

"Oh, ahh, how about over there, on that fancy little table."

"Very good, sir." After he'd set down the tray, the fat clerk headed back to the door, then stood still. His puffy pink hands sought to grip each other, not quite touching before his ample paunch, just under the jutting bottom wings of the too-tight vest.

Slocum said, "Thanks. I guess that'll do for now."

The clerk still stood there, smiling that damn smile at him. Then his eyebrows rose, his head inclined slightly.

"Oh, right . . ." Slocum dug in his denims pocket, pulled out what was in there—three spent matches, a bedraggled quirley stub, a dusting of hay chaff, and three coins, none of them together totaling a half-dollar. He pinched the dimes out of the rest, held them out, and placed them in the now-frowning fat man's palm. Slocum smiled and nodded, and the clerk offered a weak smile in return, blew the chaff from his palm, and with a head held high, exited the room.

Slocum stared at the closed door a moment, wondering how it was he'd just paid a man to do a job he'd already been paid to do. "What is the world coming to?" he mused aloud.

From the bedroom he heard a slight groan, then Ginny appeared in the doorway.

"Just in time," said Slocum. "First round arrived." He waved at the tray and offered what he hoped was a sympathetic smile.

"Oh, yes," she said, looking confused enough that Slocum thought she might take to fainting again.

"You okay, ma'am?"

"I am fine." She smiled. "Fit as a fiddle, in fact. What say we tend to that wound of yours."

Slocum suddenly wasn't interested in pretending he wanted to be there anymore. He felt bone tired, and the urge to leave appealed to him more than ever. Maybe he'd just head on out, get a stiff drink, then hit the hay.

"Again, I am so very sorry. John, was it?"

"Yep. John Slocum." They stood still for a moment, looking at each other. Slocum turned his hat in his hands. "Well, I better be going. Things to do, places to be. Good luck to you, ma'am. And if I may . . . I was you, I'd stay away from the games table. At least until you get in a bit more practice." He smiled and headed to the door.

"Mr. Slocum, please. I would like to make this up to you. I feel mortified about the unpleasantness with the hat pin . . . That it turned out the way it had."

"Well, that's water under the bridge. I'll go now."

She rushed to the door, arms spread wide, and said, "No! No, you can't go yet. We . . ." She cast her gaze around the room, saw the silver tray again, and said, "We simply must toast to our successful ouster of those ruffians."

"Yeah," he said, "but you should get some rest. You had a pretty big shock."

"Nonsense. Well, yes, but it could have been so much worse. Please, Mr. Slocum, please stay awhile at least. I . . . I'm a stranger here and I'd enjoy the company."

She offered him that charming smile again and it had the effect it had before. Maybe more so now, since he was even more tired. As if to settle the thought once and for all, he said, "Your face. It's still red. From where that man gripped you, I think."

Her hand went to her cheek. "Oh, pardon me a moment," she said. "Please pour the drinks. I'll be right back." She went into the bedroom.

Slocum did as he was bidden, mostly because the bourbon looked too good standing there to ignore, and also because if he ever needed a drink, it was now. Once he poured, he considered for the flicker of an instant whether he should be gentlemanly and wait for her. Nah, I've done my duty tonight.

He took a small pull on the whiskey, and damn, it was fine. Being a Southern boy, he was partial to a good bourbon, though how she could have known that just by sizing him up in the lobby, he didn't know. But it would be something to ask her. A way into a palaver. He'd nearly given up on any conversation with her.

She came back out of the bedroom, looking slightly less red-faced and more relaxed somehow. He guessed she had washed her face at the pitcher and bowl.

She accepted the crystal glass of champagne he offered and they clinked glasses. "To better health," he said, checking his wound. The bleeding appeared to have stopped and the sharp pain had ebbed to a dull throb.

She set down her glass and rolled up her sleeves. "We must get that shirt off you, Mr. Slocum."

"John, please, and no, I'm fine. Nothing a little bourbon and some sleep won't cure."

"No sir, I insist. I did this to you and I . . ." She broke off there, and before he knew what was happening, she'd parted his coat and begun unbuttoning his shirt.

"See here—"

"No, John Slocum. I'll not tolerate any more of your bull-headedness. Now help me slip off this coat and shirt. Oh . . ." When they caught sight of the blood, they both raised eyebrows in concern.

"I think perhaps we should send for a doctor."

"Nope. I'd be hurting a lot worse inside if I needed one."

"That's a peculiar way of looking at it."

"Peculiar situation, seems to me." He shrugged out of the

coat, then the shirt, and tossed them across the back of the stuffed wingback chair behind him.

"Mr. Slocum, your guns . . . shouldn't you take those off as well?"

"Only if they're in the way, ma'am."

"Ginny, please."

She had lightly warmed a basin of water atop the room's small stove. She carried it over to him, steam curling from the top, and dipped a washcloth in it. She downed the rest of her glass of champagne and approached him with the cloth, looking at him nervously.

He took the cloth from her, smiling, and gently dabbed the spot. "I can't even see it," he said. "No, wait, there it is—looks like a spider bite." He washed it some more, then said, "I tell you what, I've been slashed by Bowie knives, stabbed by Indian lances, shot, you name it, but this one tickled more than most."

"If you're trying to make me feel better, John Slocum, it's not working." She took the cloth from him, wrung it out, and dabbed him herself this time. "You are . . . rather scarred for so young a man."

She didn't look up at him as she bent low before him, but he could see her face redden.

She kept talking. "You are also rather fit. What I mean is . . . you look to keep yourself in good working order."

A knock at the door froze them both, as if they were children caught filching cookies from the kitchen. She set the cloth in the bowl and opened the door. "Ah, food. Good. Mr. Slocum, you must be starving."

In walked the same fat clerk from before. He glanced at the half-clad Slocum, one eyebrow arched, and his already red face nearly purpled. He cleared his throat and pushed a wheeled cart carrying several silver-domed platters. "Your . . . repast, Miss Garfield." He turned to Slocum. "Sir."

Again, he retreated to the door, hesitated, then stood before it, smiling at some spot between them.

Miss Garfield retrieved her purse, and came back with

several handsome-looking coins, which she then deposited into the man's outstretched pink hand.

"My many thanks, Miss Garfield. I hope you"—he looked briefly at Slocum—"enjoy your evening, ma'am."

He bowed and pulled the door closed quietly behind him.

"What do you suppose he meant by that?" said Slocum, knowing full well what the fat man implied, but wanting to see if he could make her blush more just the same. On her it looked especially pretty.

If she took any notice, she didn't let it show. Instead, she unscrewed the cap on a bottle of tincture, sniffed it, and wrinkled her nose. "Good Lord, what is this stuff?" She held it up for him to sniff, and he, too, recoiled. "Please don't smear that stuff on me. How about we drizzle a little of that medicinal whiskey on it and call it good."

"Nope, not that stuff," she said. "If it's as bad as the tincture, which is decidedly possible, then we're just courting disaster." She winked at him and he felt his stomach flutter. Nothing but a pretty girl ever made that happen in quite the same way.

"Now, John." She looked around the room, then grabbed the bourbon bottle by the neck and led him to the bedroom. "In there, on the bed."

"Beg your pardon?" he said, eyes wide.

"I need to drizzle some of this on your . . . wound. Okay?"

"No need to waste good bourbon."

"Plenty more where that came from, Mr. Slocum. Now, please lie back on the bed."

"Miss Garfield,"

She gave him a stern look.

"I mean, Ginny, I—"

She backed him to the bed and stood before him, hands on her hips. "That gun belt is in the way, John Slocum. I can't get at what I need to."

They stood that way, very close, her breasts touching his chest through the soft, shiny fabric of her dress. He looked down at her and knew she had to be one of the prettiest girls he'd seen in a long time, and up this close, she was even more flawless. And she smelled like spring wildflowers—lavender maybe. And in the middle of a Bismarck winter.

He felt her fingers tugging at his gun belt buckle. He helped, their eyes not leaving each other's. He held out the gun belt to his left, laid it down on the floor.

She gently pushed against his chest. He let himself fall backward onto the bed—and what a comfortable bed it was. Beat the hell out of the stable. She stood above him, hands on her hips, and that damn smile.

Now he was pretty sure he knew where this situation was headed, and he didn't mind in the least. She seemed ideal in a variety of ways—pretty, healthy, wealthy, and a sharp little thing, too (hat pins and poker-playing abilities aside), but she was a little vexing. He couldn't take the notion that she was hiding a whole lot of something. What it was, he hadn't even the first clue. But at the moment, she wasn't giving him a whole lot of chance to mull it over further.

She pushed a towel under his side, then gingerly poured bourbon onto the tiny puckered hole. It stung for a fraction of a moment, then felt fine. She held the bottle up and peered close to the wound, concern wrinkling her brow. Slocum took the bottle from her hand and propped himself up on an elbow. He swallowed back a leisurely couple of jolts. "You should be a nurse, Ginny. You have a fine bedside manner."

She smiled up at him, a mischievous arch to her eyebrows. "Who says I'm not? I'm not satisfied yet with the job."

She unfastened the top few buttons of his fly and eased the waistband of his denims down to expose more of his side. Then she took the bottle from him and began to drizzle more of the whiskey on his side.

"I think you about got it," said Slocum, still propped on his elbow.

"No, no I don't believe so." Without looking at him, she gently pushed against his chest and he lay flat again. Then he felt her hands working the rest of his fly and a gasp from her as she freed him. He was already there, full-masted and tight-to-the-hide. He swore he heard her whisper, "Oh my word," and he closed his eyes, smiling despite himself.

He heard a slight rustling, then a gurgling sound, then a gentle clunk as if she'd set the bourbon bottle down on the floor. He wanted to look at the proceedings, but didn't want to interrupt her, lest she grow self-conscious.

Then he was surprised by the sudden touch of something right on the very tip of his member. Something moist that parted and slipped down over it, numbing it within seconds and wetting it at the same time. He looked then, and saw her staring up at him, kneeling before him, her shoulders bare, and her mouth wrapped around him, and what felt like bourbon slowly drizzling out of her mouth onto the length of him. And it felt amazing. He collapsed flat on the bed again. His breath stuttered, then leaked out of him as if he'd been deflated.

Soon, she began to work him up and down, slowly at first, and even through the slight numbness he felt the edges of her teeth graze him. She paused, explored him all around with her searching tongue, then continued faster. She did the same down lower on his shaft, then beneath, where she cupped and kissed him slowly, then trailed back up to the tip. She opened her mouth and let go of him for a moment, but he guessed she might work her way upward—which she did.

Gentle kisses trailed up from his root, zigzagging, and pausing near his hat pin puncture, where she ever so gently licked and kissed him in the general region. He didn't even flinch. Her hair was no longer piled on her head but loose. He knew because he felt it tickling him as she worked her way up his body.

Then she made her way upward to his chest, neck, chin, then mouth, and he could smell the musky bourbon of her breath.

As she lay on top of him, he felt her entire body, every hill and valley. He felt her pert, full breasts squash flat against him, felt her heart hammering in her smooth-skinned chest. He wrapped his arms around her and pulled her tightly to him, felt her legs part and he slipped in between them, her warmth and wetness inviting. She raised her hips up, up just high enough, wiggled them, and then he felt one hand reach down, grip him, and guide him in.

She slid down the length of him slowly, her breath draining out of her. On his face it felt like a warm breeze on a hot summer day. She sat up, fully impaled on him, and only then did he look at her. Her long tresses hung silky and luminescent in the dimmed lamp glow of the room.

She was careful not to let her leg rub against his side, and for that he was grateful—it was still a mite tender. She rode him gently but firmly, clasping him tight with each rise up and down, as if massaging him with unseen hands. Her eyes were half-lidded, and her hair bounced on her firm breasts and pert nipples.

Slocum could resist no longer and gently caressed them, thumbing the scarlet nibs until they were like pebbles under his hands. She moaned soft noises in the back of her throat, and he pushed his palms against her breasts, gently massaging in a circular motion, and her riding became more strident.

Then she did a strange thing—she just stopped, stared at him as if she'd just remembered something going on in the next room, and smiled. She raised herself up, and without rising fully off him, she lifted one slender leg, placed the knee, and did the same with her other leg until she was facing away from him.

Slocum grabbed her perfect hips, sandwiching that pert backside between his hands, and scooched backward to the middle of the bed. And tried to accommodate her by kneeling, but she was having none of it. She gently but firmly eased him back down and resumed her ride, this time facing away from him. He watched the long, muscled plane of her back arch, traced the valley of her spine up to where it disappeared beneath her long hair. She leaned back until she was almost laid out on top of him, her arms planted on either side of his chest, her hair partially in his face, but he didn't care. He massaged her breasts, inducing more moans until it seemed she couldn't stand it. She rose up again, only to keep going, and planted herself on all fours before him. This time he sat up, managed to slide his legs out from under hers, and knelt behind her.

He gripped her about the waist, slid one hand across her belly, and massaged her just where they met. She cried out as he set up a rhythm that would brook no more changes in the program. And judging from the enthusiastic response he received, she didn't want it any other way.

For long minutes they worked together, harder and faster, sustaining an intensity and rhythm that he'd not experienced in a long time. She was a vigorous partner, and he worked to match her enthusiasm stroke for stroke. Soon, though, they both sensed something in the other—a tightening and urgent heightening of pleasure that was undeniable.

They both quickened their paces and, trembling, released a pent-up urgency that held them atop the crest of their sweat-laden wave but a few breathless moments before succumbing to near exhaustion.

She sagged against him, and he to her. She offered a quiet sigh, the only sound other than their heavy breathing.

Twenty minutes later found them both sitting up in bed, silver trays balanced on their knees, and each hungrily slicing into steaks, potatoes, salads, and vegetables, which were still surprisingly warm—and cooked, in Slocum's estimation, to perfection.

After a few minutes he noticed she had stopped eating and was staring at him. He paused, his mouth full of delicious steak. "What's wrong?"

She smiled, ran a hand through her hair, and rested an elbow on her knee. "It's been a while since I've seen a man eat. I mean, really eat. You seem to be enjoying yourself."

He felt a little self-conscious. He knew he had decent manners, but the notion of a woman sitting there watching him eat made him feel a little odd. "How long have you been watching me anyway?" he said, wiping his mouth with the cloth napkin.

"Just a minute. I'm stuffed, but you should keep on going. I'm serious, there's plenty more."

"More of what?" he smirked. It turned into a smile when he heard her throaty laugh.

"You, John Slocum, are a rogue. You have nearly tuckered me out, truth be told."

"Nearly?" he said, pouring himself another sip of bourbon.

She set her tray on the bedside table. "Nearly, sir. But not wholly. Not yet." She laid a hand on his belly, then it disappeared beneath the sheets, and within seconds the sheets rose.

"Care for dessert?" she said.

He set his own dishes on the floor and said, "I do believe I could nibble on a little something."

Slocum awoke early the next morning, light angling in through a crack in the drawn drapes, his head throbbing lightly. But what woke him were a couple of short cries of shock.

"What's wrong?"

"Oh, oh . . . oh my God!"

He sat up, wondering what in the hell he was in the midst of, fragments of the previous evening coming back to him. Despite his pulsing temples, he recalled it all with a growing grin. "Ginny? What's wrong?"

She was seated at the little mirror-backed table where ladies put on their face, staring into the mirror with a look of mortified horror on her pretty face. She had her hands on her ears and turned to him as he came up behind her. "John," she said, "when we . . . you know, were . . . enjoying ourselves, did you happen to notice if I was wearing . . . anything?"

He put a hand on her shoulder, smoothed her soft hair, and admired her bare naked reflection in the mirror. "Girl, as I recall, you weren't wearing a thing but a smile."

Her consternation broke down for a moment, and a small smile lit her pretty face. "Mighty big talk, Mr. Slocum."

"Am I wrong?"

"Not at all." Her smile faded. "But John, I need you to think back. Do you remember me wearing both earrings back here last night? I have to know." She held up one dangling, diamond-laden earring. "They're my grandmother's and they've been in the Garfield family for a long, long time."

He whistled long and low. "Let's see now." He sat on the bed, doing his best to recall what had happened before the most interesting events of the prior evening began. "No, no, I definitely remember you wearing, well, at least one earring. And the necklace and that thing on your wrist, as well."

He looked at her when she didn't respond—and saw tears welling in her eyes. He reached for his denims. "You search here, I'll go out in the street, trace our steps back to where the scuffle took place. It's early enough that not many folks will have been up, and I don't think we were due to get any more snow. If you find it, sit tight. I'll be back. If I find it, I'll be back soon. Okay?" He smiled and paused, tugging on his shirt as she hugged him.

"Thank you, John. I know it's silly, but—"

"No need to explain. If it means that much to you, it's worth putting in a little effort over, right?"

She nodded and tugged on a dressing gown, already turning from him to rummage in her belongings once again.

He strapped on his guns and headed out of the bedroom to the front room.

"You will be back, John?"

He nodded. "Count on it. With any luck, maybe we can have a bit of celebratory breakfast." He left the room, tugged on his hat, and headed down the stairs. He half expected to see the fat man at the desk, but he must have been off duty. A middle-aged woman with a bitter, pruned face looked up from a novel she was reading and eyed him. Might as well have a little fun, he thought, and stepped over to the desk. "Good morning, ma'am. I'm a friend of Miss Garfield. I'll be back in a little while. Need to take in the air."

He walked toward the door, waiting to hear her make some remark about the impropriety of it all, but when he glanced back as he opened the door, she was still reading her book. However, this time there was a smile on her face. Maybe it's a romantic tale, he thought.

As he let his eyes adjust to the bright sun reflecting off the snow, he noticed with relief that he'd been correct—no new snow had fallen overnight. He also didn't see any other folks out and about yet. Good. He bent low and studied the sidewalk, then the ground all the way to the spot where they'd tussled. It was easy to locate as the footprints, the scuffed gravel and dirt, and the churned clots of snow were all plainly visible.

He bent low and only then did he recall being stuck with her hat pin the evening before. He reached under his coat, probed the spot on his side, and was relieved to find it barely hurt at all. Just a harmless puncture, he thought. Surely if something had been damaged inside, he'd know by now. He vowed, however, to steer clear of hat-wearing women in distress.

Slocum's breath rose up in plumes, and as he toed the dirty snow out of the way, he found nothing. He widened the search area into the snow where she'd fallen, but still found nothing. He was about to head up the steps to the saloon, see if maybe it was wedged in a gap in the boards. He stopped to tug on his leather gloves and noticed movement out of the corner of his eye. It came from down the street toward the livery, where he would have spent the night with his horse, the Appaloosa, had Miss Garfield not tried her hand at gambling.

He almost ignored it, wanting to inspect the walk up to the saloon door, lest someone else get there ahead of him, but something made him look twice. And he was glad he did.

Several buildings down, walking toward him along his side of the street, were the two men who had assaulted Ginny Garfield the night before. The short blond man in the rough cap strode along beside the tall, rat-faced man. But they hadn't yet seen him. They were staring hard at something the blond was holding. They were also murmuring low, the still, morning street affording Slocum little chance to move without being seen.

He backed close to the edge of the saloon front, ducking down, the elevated walk nearly chest high, and waited for them to approach. He would have a talk with these ruffians. And maybe a little more, now that they were on equal footing.

He risked a glance up and back toward them. They had stopped and were admiring whatever it was the man held in his hands. The object of their attention glinted, caught a ray of light, and shone for a fraction of a moment, reflecting into a dozen brilliant colors at once. The diamond earring! Had to be. But they still weren't moving, just standing there, admiring the thing. He had to do something, had to get it back. They were still too far away for him to bolt after—there was enough distance between them that they might well outrun him.

He looked behind him, saw the alley, and another just behind them. Perfect. He would have to cross about six feet of open ground before he'd be hidden by the near alley. He shucked a pistol, just in case he was seen and had to draw on them instead. And he went for it—straight into the mouth of the alley, one eye on them the entire time. They never looked up, not even when his boot heel caught on the edge of the sidewalk as he stepped off.

He staggered a bit in the alley, righted himself, and cat-footed around the building they were in front of, then up the alley behind them. Just before he eased to the mouth of the alley, he raised the pistol up chest height, and just as he was about to step out onto the boardwalk, he heard them resume walking—drawing closer. Their murmuring, though still unintelligible to him, sounded excited and even giddy. He'd soon put a stop to that.

At the last second, he holstered his Colt and raised his arms. Just as they slow-walked before the mouth of the alley, he reached out and grabbed each of them by the coat collar and dragged them backward

"Aaah!" said the blond man, but the rat-faced man went down like a dropped plank, and immediately curled up into a ball. Slocum planted a boot on his chest and set to work on the smaller man while he still had the element of surprise in his favor.

"What the hell?" The blond thrashed on his back, looking around the still-dark alley, wondering just what had happened to him, when Slocum planted the first punch on the kid's jaw. It didn't knock him cold, but it did daze him and shut him up.

Slocum leaned low over the kid's face. "Remember me, you little jackass?"

The kid blinked hard, shook his head, then his eyes grew wide in recognition. "Oh God, mister, I . . ."

"Save it for the marshal." He lifted his boot off Rat Face's chest and smacked the man with a short, sharp backhand to the temple. "You stay put." Then he turned his attention back to the smaller man. "Now, what's that in your hand?"

The kid balled his hands tight at the question.

"No, no, no. That's no way to answer me, fella. See, I asked you a question, and you had better answer by showing me what you have there, or I'm liable to really make your life . . . painful." With that Slocum slid his big Bowie knife free of its hip sheath.

"Oh God!" said the kid again.

"I don't think he much cares about you right now, kid." Slocum dragged the needle-like tip of the blade across the kid's swallowing throat. "Now, about that hand."

"You promise not to hurt me?"

"Hey . . ." Rat Face said.

"Us, I mean. You promise?"

"I make no promises to scum like you. But I will take it into consideration. That's the best you'll get from me. Take it or leave it."

The blond swallowed again, then nodded, his eyes wide in fear. But there was still something there that Slocum recognized from the countless times he'd had to deal with scum like him. It was the glimmer of anger, the recklessness of a youth thinking he could come out on top in any situation. Not a bad trait to have, but not a good one in this instance.

Slocum sighed and backhanded the kid across the chops.

"Don't," he said, pointing a long, straight finger right at the kid's nose.

"Don't what? What was that for?"

"For thinking what you were thinking. Just don't do it."

"You're crazy, mister."

"Yep." Beside Slocum, Rat Face shifted on the ground. Slocum drove his boot against the man again to settle him. "And I'm the one with the knife, two guns, and I also didn't attack a woman just last night either. So what's it going to be from you?"

The kid seemed to tense solid for a few moments, eyes sparking, but then he sagged, the fire of anger having dulled in him.

"The hand."

The kid raised his hand and opened it—and there in the faint but growing light in the alleyway, Slocum saw the twin earring to Ginny's. He took it, dropped it into his coat pocket, and said, "I'm about to make a young woman very happy. And you two men are about to become very sad."

"What? Why?" said the blond kid.

"Because you both are going to visit the marshal, which should come as no surprise to you."

"Aw, no, don't do that," said Rat Face.

"Why shouldn't I? You assaulted an innocent young woman with the intention of robbing her—and you succeeded in doing just that." He patted his pocket. "And there's the proof."

"Yeah, but she ain't what she lets on she is. You know?"

Slocum played it as if he were not unaware of what the man was saying. "Might be I do. Fill me in with what you know and I'll consider your options."

Rat Face started to speak, but the blond kid cut him off. "Shut your mouth, dammit. We ain't gotta tell him anything."

Slocum grabbed the blond's shirtfront and raised him up until they were staring at each other but an inch apart.

"Yeah," he said through clenched teeth. "You do." He tuned to Rat Face. "Now speak."

Rat Face swallowed, his Adam's apple bobbing. "That rich girl, she was here looking for a fella. Sure as shootin'."

"How do you know that?" said Slocum.

"Because . . ."

But the blond made another sound and Slocum tightened his grip on the young man's collar. "You were saying?"

Rat Face continued, "The man she's after was here in Bismarck, a few days back. He told us to keep an eye out for her. Told us what she looked like. Said that we should keep her from following him somehow, and if we did, then he would pay us a lot of money."

The blond chimed in. "And that he was on special orders from the government."

"And you both believed him?"

The two hoodlums exchanged glances. "Well, of course," said Rat Face, as if Slocum had just asked him if it was winter in North Dakota.

Slocum sighed, relaxed his grip on the blond's shirtfront. "Did this man say why she would be looking for him?"

"Naw, just that she needed to be stopped, any way we saw fit. But he made it pretty plain that we should . . . you know . . . kill her."

"Kill her? Is that what you two were going to do last night if I hadn't come along?"

"No!" They both said it at the same time. "We knew it was her when she come to town on the train. Then we saw all that money and thought that if we just took her money, she wouldn't have no way to follow him on account of her being broke and all."

He said it in such a way that Slocum felt pretty sure they weren't killers. Not yet anyway. He'd seen small-time crooks become murderers as they grew older and more desperate.

"This man, did he have a name?"

They both shook their heads. "Not that we ever heard," said Rat Face.

"What did he look like?"

"Oh, he was tall as you, but had light-colored hair, like

his," said Rat Face, pointing to his cohort, who sneered at him. "And a big waxy mustache. He dressed like a dandy, too. Nice clothes and all, you know?"

"Except dandies don't just light a shuck on out of town in winter on horseback for no reason, now do they?" The blond sneered, staring his friend down, as if he'd trumped him at something.

"Do you know where he was headed?" said Slocum.

"I'd say he was headed north." Rat Face said it with conviction.

"West," said the blond kid, shaking his head.

"Which is it?" said Slocum, narrowing his eyes at them.

"Both, really," said Rat Face.

"And how do you know that?"

"Because we watched him ride on out of town with his horse sort of loaded down with supplies."

Slocum thought about all this for a moment, then said, "Tell you both what I'm going to do. I'm not going to turn you in to the marshal . . . yet. But if I ever hear tell of either of you—and I never forget a face—causing havoc or molesting anyone, especially a woman again, I will track you down and gut you, skin you, then tack your hides to the nearest barn wall to dry. You got my meaning?"

Rat Face nodded, his Adam's apple working hard as he swallowed.

"Both of you?"

The blond had conjured up his spiteful demeanor again. "You don't scare me none."

"I was you, I'd reconsider what you're saying." Slocum bent low again, but spoke loud enough for them both to hear. "To a government operative. You'll only ever get the one chance from me. Then you are done and cooked."

He stood up, slid the knife back into its sheath. "Do we understand each other, gentlemen? One more slipup and you had better pray the marshal gets to you before I do. Of course, there isn't a cell made that I can't get into or out of."

They both swallowed then, and began scooching away

from him. He touched his hat brim. "Good day, gentlemen."
He stepped out of the alley and headed to the hotel, resisting
the urge to smile until he was well out of sight of the two
hellions.

Now he needed some answers from Miss Ginny Garfield.

3

Slocum knocked, then entered her rooms, peeling off his coat. "Ginny? You here?"

She had spiffed up the room, aired it out, for the air felt fresh and bracing, and the little stove was working overtime to raise the temperature again to a comfortable level. On the table in the sitting room, a fresh silver tray sat covered in gleaming dishes, with a coffee urn in the midst of it. He'd smelled it as he'd walked up the stairs and hoped she'd ordered some. His head was still throbbing like cannonfire, but he was happy.

"John, I . . . Did you find it? Did you find my grandmother's earring?"

He retrieved it from his pocket and held it toward her. "Yep," he said, not bothering to tone down his smile.

She was so happy that she hugged him. "Oh, thank you, John. This is incredible. Where was it?"

"Oh, out on the sidewalk."

He sipped the coffee. It was strong and had a slightly bitter edge to it, just the way he liked it. Hell, who was he kidding? He liked anything resembling coffee. "So, who is this handsome blond man you're following?"

Her face immediately lost its color, and for a second he thought she was going to faint again.

"Ginny? You okay?"

She looked at him. "Is he here? In town?"

"Is who here, Ginny? Tell me what's going on."

She grabbed Slocum's arms. "Is he here? I have to know."

Slocum regarded her eyes a moment. There was plenty of fire there, and desperation, too. "He left days ago, was seen headed sort of northwest out of town."

Her face fell.

"Ginny, what's this all about? Maybe I can help."

She looked at the earring in her hand, wiped away a tear sliding down her cheek, and said, "No, you've done enough already."

He sipped his coffee. "I'm not leaving until you tell me what's going on. Why are you here in Bismarck of all places, and in midwinter? A more unforgiving place you'll not find. I know," he chuckled. "I've been trying to leave for months now."

She turned to him, her face suddenly hopeful. "You have?"

"Well, yeah. I've been waiting for the weather to break, then I'm heading south and I'm not going to stop until I begin to sweat." He smiled, but her face lost its glow.

"Oh, yes, a good plan. It is cold here." And then she began to sob.

He took her in his arms and, after a few moments, said, "Look, Ginny. I have no idea what's going on with you, but I do know it can't hurt to tell me. Hell, it might just help."

She nodded and sat down across the table from him, drying her eyes on a handkerchief. Slocum uncovered the breakfast dishes and served them each a big plateful of eggs, toasted bread, sliced apples and cream, butter, bacon, sausage, and more coffee. The food seemed to help get her talking, and she kept right on talking even in between bites, not worrying about appearing ladylike in the least.

"The man I'm looking for is named Delbert Calkins. He's

the worst of the worst. A scoundrel and a rogue and a cheat, and a liar and . . ."

"Bad man, huh?" said Slocum, smiling.

But she didn't match his smile, just looked at him. "John, he killed my brother."

"Oh, I am truly sorry, Ginny."

"It takes a while to get over."

"How long has it been?"

"Less than a year, but I've only been looking for him for a couple of months."

He leaned back. "Why don't you start at the beginning, as they say. Tell me about it. Maybe I can help."

"Is that what you do, John? Funny but I never thought to ask much about you." She smiled. "I just assumed the worst and stabbed you."

"I've been treated worse. Now, about this Delbert fellow."

"Well, let's see. The beginning . . . My father is Gilbert G. Garfield." She regarded him a moment as if to let that tidbit of information sink in.

"I gather I'm supposed to be impressed," he said. "But I am going to disappoint you."

She looked a little annoyed and he supposed that was the spoiled rich girl in her coming out. "We're the Garfields of Garfield Coal, Trains . . . Shipping."

"What a coincidence. I'm a Slocum of . . . me and my horse and saddle."

"Okay, I understand I may have come across as boorish. I can't help it if my family has a little money."

He raised his eyebrows.

"We're wealthy. Very wealthy," she said.

"So . . . Bismarck?"

She exhaled deeply and said, "Delbert was or rather *is* an unsavory sort. Not the type my father would approve of. But maybe because of that fact, I became attracted to Delbert. I don't really want to admit it, but he is handsome."

"In a roguish sort of way," said Slocum.

"You should know, sir." She smiled, lost it quickly, and resumed. "Anyway, we met one day when I was down near the docks, sketching for an art class I was taking at the University. Oh, we're from Chicago. And he just came up behind me, carrying a couple of bags of seed in burlap sacks on his shoulders, and told me that although it was obvious I had talent, I was too heavy-handed with my use of umber. And do you know? He was right. I started going down there more frequently, under the pretense of sketching, but I always managed to bump into Delbert Calkins, oddly enough."

"Imagine that," said Slocum. "And then one thing led to another."

"Yes, it was a bit of a whirlwind courtship."

"I can see where this is headed," he said. "And it ain't pretty, I'll bet."

"How right you are. I invited Delbert to our house."

"Mansion?"

"Yes, mansion. May I finish my story?" She sipped her coffee and Slocum followed suit, said nothing, but waved his hand for her to continue.

"Daddy was most displeased that Delbert should even be allowed into the house, let alone court his daughter . . ." She fell silent a moment, then said, "I won't bore you with the sordid details, but I can assure you that I am as headstrong as he is. And more than my brother, too. He is, was, Gilbert G. Garfield the Second, though we always called him Jamie. He was younger than me by two years, and was forever trying to make Daddy proud of him, doing things that would get Daddy's attention. But I'm afraid Daddy just ignored his attempts and considered Jamie a silly little boy, even though he was really quite gifted with figures. I daresay he would have filled in for Daddy quite well. But all that's too late now. Such speculation is fruitless."

Slocum didn't say a word, just let her gather her thoughts and continue.

"I persisted in seeing much more of Delbert Calkins, and though he was a bit rough on the outside, he was a kind young man. Or so I thought. Unbeknownst to me, my brother had been following him, spying on him, and for once he did something that pleased my father. Jamie found out that Delbert was part of a gang of criminals that preyed on the wealthy by endearing themselves to them, getting invited into their homes. Sometimes even becoming members of their families."

"Was that something you and Delbert had discussed? Marriage?"

She said nothing, merely nodded, but couldn't meet his gaze.

"He came over one night, and we had agreed that he would meet with my father in his study, to ask for my hand in marriage. Father, of course, had no idea this was to take place. I was upstairs, getting fancied up in my best dress and my grandmother's jewels, which you've seen, when my brother knocked on my door. He asked to see me. I could tell he was angry about something, but I was in too good a mood to pay his demeanor much heed. He asked me why I was so happy and I just blurted it out—that Delbert was downstairs right then asking Daddy for my hand in marriage.

"I don't know what I expected. Jamie had made it plain that he did not care for Delbert in the least. But he grew so furious, such an anger as I'd never seen on him before. He told me in no uncertain terms just what he thought of Delbert, and he used words that would make a sailor blush. He also told me what he said he'd found out about having Delbert followed for weeks on behalf of Daddy.

"He reduced me to tears, then bounded down the stairs shouting that he had to put an end to the madness once and for all. What that meant, I had no idea. I shouted at him as he ran from my room that . . . Oh, John! I told him I hated him, that I wished him dead for what he was about to do. Can you imagine? Oh, those words still echo in my head. They were the last words I would ever speak to dear Jamie."

She sat still for a few quiet moments, then wiped her eyes and continued.

"By the time I got downstairs to Daddy's study, I could hear two voices shouting within the closed doors—my brother arguing with Delbert, and Delbert not refuting the same accusations my brother had shouted at me moment before upstairs—not one bit! But then Delbert told my brother that he and my father had already settled the situation. I remember there was a pause then, and Jamie asked him what he meant by that.

"I almost barged in, but something stayed my hand. I had to hear what Delbert was about to say. Would that I had entered the room! Oh, I'm such a fool. What shocked me the most was Delbert's voice saying what hypocrites all wealthy people were. That they liked to make a hue and cry out of honor and justice. Oh, he'd said he appreciated the fire and verve my brother was showing, but that all rich folks really care about was money. He said that at least he was being honest. Jamie had asked him what he meant by that and Delbert said that my father had offered him ten thousand dollars in cash to leave and never be heard from again."

Slocum whistled low. "And Delbert accepted?"

"Yes, damn his black soul." She hastily wiped away a tear threatening to undermine her anger. "I heard him say something like, 'Here it is, in my hand. And don't think the matter ends here. Oh, no, no, no. I'll be back for more. This is just a down payment, you can rest assured."

Ginny paused, rubbed her eyes.

Slocum sensed she was building up to something especially difficult for her to give voice to, so he kept quiet.

"Then he said, 'I've got that silly little sister of yours wrapped right around my finger. She'll do anything for me. Hmm, I wonder how much dear old Daddy will pay to prevent an elopement? Or maybe I should just marry the little fool and beget a whole new branch of the family tree!' "

"I imagine your brother didn't take that too well. Where was your father in all this?"

"He told me later that he left the room when Jamie showed up. Was beside himself and ashamed, too. He said he'd never forgive himself, but that he'd suddenly taken ill at what he'd done and had to . . . well, upheave, if you know what I mean."

"I understand—and I guess I'd be inclined to do the same if I'd just given in to a blackmailer's demands."

"Jamie howled his outrage then, and I tried to open the door, but someone, maybe Jamie, had locked it from the inside. I heard him shout, 'You foul villain! The only way you'll leave this room is over my dead body!' And Delbert laughed—he actually laughed! Then he . . . he said he would be happy to accommodate him and . . . he shot Jamie!

I banged on the door and within seconds it swung inward and there stood Delbert, smiling at me and tucking something into his coat."

"Was it the pistol?" said Slocum.

She shook her head. "At least not that I saw. There was a pistol in my brother's hand as he lay on the floor. I saw him lying there and yelled, 'What did you do?' to Delbert. Still smiling, he shrugged and said, 'A clear-cut case of self-defense, m'lady.' He always called me that. Like a fool, I'd thought it was cute, but now I realize he had been mocking me all along.

" 'Pity,' Delbert had said. 'I would have liked to have had . . . those jewels. Another time, perhaps, you poor little rich girl.' Then he turned and ran out the front door, knocking over servants in the process."

"What about chasing after him? Did no one pursue him? Call the law and track him?"

"Oh, I wanted to, believe me. As did the servants, and others. But you have to understand, my father is . . ."

"Very wealthy, yes you said. And I bet he's also afraid to go to the law because it might tarnish his business reputation." Slocum poured himself another cup of coffee. "So you don't know for certain if Delbert shot your brother without much provocation, or if Jamie threatened him with a gun first."

"Well, no, I don't know. But I swear he planted the gun in Jamie's hand to make it look like he'd been defending himself."

"Makes sense, but you didn't actually see Delbert pocket his gun."

She shook her head no.

"And did anybody check to see if the pistol in your brother's hand had been fired? Sniff it, check the chambers, the barrel?"

"Of course it had been fired! It was the one Delbert used to shoot him. Honestly."

"Now don't get all worked up. I'm trying to make a point. If it hadn't been fired, then you'd have no case against the man because it could be said that Jamie had drawn on him, but Delbert beat him to the trigger, then pocketed his own pistol."

She stared at him for a moment, then realization dawned on her face. "So simple, but we never thought of it. At least my father never said if he did. How foolish of me."

"So, where does that leave you? I am guessing you didn't prosecute him, especially given the fact that you're chasing him across the country."

"As I said before, my family is wealthy and Daddy didn't want to air family laundry in public, especially given the fact that blackmail was involved and that he paid the man. Imagine what that would do to his business reputation. He told me he'd be laughed out of every negotiation."

"I take it your father is known as a hard hand in such matters."

She nodded. "He says it's the only way to succeed in business."

"Well," said Slocum, "it sure is one way, he's proven that. But did he do anything about it? Ever try to find the man?"

"He told me he had hired a private firm to take care of matters, that's what he called it."

"But . . ." Slocum prompted her.

She sighed. "But I was snooping around in the papers on his desk one day, because I had my doubts, and, well, let's just say that I found out he had never hired anybody to do anything."

"So you took matters into your own hands, and took to the road, trying to find this man."

"Yes. I've kept in touch with Daddy, told him not to worry. But in truth, he knows I'm most capable of handling myself."

Slocum's raised eyebrows made her look down at her lap.

"Well, I thought I was. Until you saved me from those two ruffians. And then I stabbed you! Oh, what a mess I've made of things. I wish I never had met that damnable Delbert Calkins. Don't you see?" She looked up at him, tears in her eyes again. "I am responsible for all of it. For my brother's death, for my father's recent dark humors. The man has always been a kind soul, full of jollity and good humor. But lately he has taken to brooding alone in his study, the very room Jamie died in. Oh, it's all my fault."

"So you're tailing a killer across the country to make up for it. Admirable, I'll give you that. But what's your plan?"

"What do you mean?"

"Did you really think that playing poker in Bismarck in the middle of a hard winter among rough and shaggy characters would help?" He shook his head in disbelief at the poor girl.

"I have employed several operatives to help me track him. They told me that all along he has been gambling in every town he stops at. The last town I had word of his appearance was here in Bismarck. That was two weeks ago. I hurried to get here, but it seems I was too late. I thought that if I confronted him, he might . . ."

"What? Surrender? Repent and beg your forgiveness?" Slocum stood and stalked the room. This girl was naïve and unbelievable. "Delbert Calkins was born bad, he'll live bad, and he'll die bad. You have my word on that. I've met enough such characters that I'd wager my last two cents on it."

"You think I don't know that? It doesn't mean I'm giving up. I'll track him to the ends of the earth."

"And then what, Ginny? Will you shoot him?"

"Maybe I will." She pulled open her purse and slid out a two-shot lady's pistol, gold-plated with ivory handles.

"Cute," said Slocum. "You get close enough and you might cause him to bleed out, but there's a lot of ifs to overcome before that can happen."

"What do you suggest?"

"I suggest you go home, consider Bismarck the closest call you'll ever want to have, and leave it alone. It's a small price to pay for your foolish actions—you could have easily been killed. If he ever comes back into your life, swallow your wealthy pride and call the law. They are more than equipped to handle such a worthless bum."

The room was quiet for a time. Finally she slipped the pistol back into her purse and set it on the table by her elbow. "Then you find him." She pulled out a wad of cash and a fancy sack heavy with coins and set them on the table. "I can pay whatever you want."

Slocum rolled his eyes. "Ginny, it's not about money. I'm not—"

"John, I have no one else to turn to, and if you don't take on the job, I will go on myself. You said so yourself that he was seen mere days ago heading northwest out of Bismarck. That's good enough for me."

He wished he'd had the good sense to keep his damn mouth shut. "You'll die out there. Winter travel is no joke. Even for experienced folks, it can be an easy, sometimes a surefire way to lose your life."

"But you didn't say no."

"No, no I didn't." He pulled on his hat, tugged it down low. "I have to go check on my horse, take a walk."

"But—"

"I'll think about it." He left, closing the door behind him and pausing in the hallway. What a mess. Heading northwest in the middle of February was the last thing he wanted to do. Leaving Bismarck behind would be welcome, sure. Nice enough town, but he'd grown stale here. He wanted to be alone again, depending on himself. But northwest? And in winter? That bore serious thought.

And yet, and he hated himself for thinking it, there was

money to be made here, and it wouldn't be wrong to take it from her, since it might well be saving her life. He didn't doubt for one minute that she was headstrong enough to chase after Delbert Calkins herself. The man had probably killed her brother, wronged her in a bad emotional way, and gutted their family—not to mention that he blackmailed them and threatened more of the same. And part of a gang of criminals, she'd called it. Vermin, more like it. Slocum also didn't doubt her sincerity. He was rarely wrong about judging people, and guessed she was as honest as the day was long.

By then he'd made it to the lobby. He looked up at the front desk and saw the same pinch-faced woman holding the same novel . . . and smiling at him. He smiled back and circled the big settee in the middle of the room, headed back up the stairs.

He opened the door to her rooms, didn't see her, and strode to the bedroom. "I'll track him for you, but on a few conditions."

He'd surprised her—she was packing her things.

"What are you doing?"

"Packing. I didn't think I'd ever see you again."

"I told you I'd be back, didn't I?"

"Yes, but . . ."

"Don't tell me rich people don't believe in keeping their word?"

It was a flinty thing of him to say, but she took it well, and smiled for the first time in an hour.

"What are your conditions, Mr. Slocum?" she said, smiling that damn smile at him from where she stood at the foot of the bed.

"That you promise me you'll head back to Chicago right away and wait to hear from me. It might take a while, so be patient. Also, you have to promise me that you won't wear your grandmother's jewels again until you get home, and that you won't gamble. You are, without a doubt, the worst poker player I've ever met."

She canted her head to the side, pretended to muse on his

conditions, then said, "Called your bluff, didn't I?" Then she pushed the stack of clothing off the bed, jumped backward onto it, and lay there on her back, smiling up at him.

There's that damn smile, he thought, tossing his hat onto a chair.

4

Later that day, Slocum finally tore himself away from the amorous attentions of Ginny Garfield, armed with a wad of cash she insisted he take to help outfit himself for the hard weather and harder work ahead. His first stop was the livery where he'd kept his Appaloosa stallion since coming to Bismarck. He'd kept the horse exercised regularly, but the big beast was clearly annoyed with him, nipping and trying to take a chunk out of him every time Slocum even looked like he was about to turn away.

"One more time, damn you, and there will be hell to pay." He pointed his finger in the horse's face a moment longer for emphasis and the horse jerked for it as if it were a carrot. He rapped the beast hard once on its rubbery nose and turned it loose into the paddock for a quick romp. "Enjoy your freedom now, dang you, because we're hitting the trail in about an hour."

He paid old Mose, the ancient black man in charge of the livery, the four dollars he owed him, plus ten extra. "Just for yourself, Mose. For your help and kindness."

"Why, Mr. Slocum, way you're talkin', I'd say you're fixing to skedaddle from these parts." He leaned close and smiled. "Someplace warm, I bet, and with all manner of ladies in pretty colored dresses, huh?"

Slocum shook his head, smiling. "Wish I could say that was true, Mose. But it's northwest for me, I'm afraid. And that leads me to another question I have for you—I'll need a packhorse. Something strong, not afraid of the cold, good wind, but chesty for mountain travel."

"Northwest of here ain't too mountainous, if you'll pardon me for saying so."

"I understand, but I have to be prepared, just in case. The Rockies are a ways away, but you never know. And besides, if a horse is good going uphill, he should be solid on flat ground, right?"

The old man chuckled. "I reckon that's some sort of logic to what you're saying." He shook his head. "I'll go fetch a couple for you to look at."

"No need. I have to attend to a few things, be back inside an hour. But I trust your judgment, Mose. And your price. Just make sure it's solid and that's good enough for me." In truth, in the few weeks Slocum had been in somewhat residence at the livery, helping the old man when time—and Mose— allowed, Slocum had seen few people who could better the man at judging or tending horseflesh. Mose seemed born to the task, as an old-timer once said of especially skilled people.

"Well, Mr. Slocum, that's mighty kind of you to say. I won't steer you wrong."

Then a thought occurred to him: Maybe Mose recalled seeing Delbert Calkins. The man must have kept a low and quiet appearance, because Slocum couldn't place him at all. "Mose, you recall seeing a man, probably dandied up, the gambling sort, blond hair, fancy mustache, went by the name of Delbert Calkins?"

"When would this have been?"

"Oh, a few days or more ago."

"Don't ring no bells, but Bismarck's a big town, you know."

Slocum nodded. "Well, thanks just the same. I'll be back within the hour to load up my gear."

"I'll have a right good packhorse and that high-steppin' Appy ready and waitin'."

"I appreciate it, Mose. And watch him," said Slocum over his shoulder. "He's a devil."

"Ain't a bedeviled horse yet old Mose ain't worked the starch out of."

Slocum laughed and nodded in agreement as he headed on up the street to the mercantile. He spent ten minutes placing a decent order for goods he'd need on the trail. He figured to shoot his meat once he got out there, but he'd also bring along salt pork, beans, plenty of Arbuckle's so he wouldn't have to roast green coffee beans, plus flour, salt, several sacks of dried fruit and jerked meat, and a stack of boxes of ammunition for his Colt Navy side arms and his Winchester rifle. He added to that a few sacks of tobacco, rolling papers, three boxes of lucifers—handier than flint on steel—plus lacing and needles to repair saddles and gear. Damage to such items was inevitable.

The shopkeep, a man he'd come to a nodding acquaintance with since he had arrived in town, looked as though he wanted to inquire as to Slocum's business, since it was obvious that Slocum was preparing for a trip of some sort. But the man was older, and one who minded his business until he was told of others'.

Slocum was about to repeat the question he'd asked Mose about Delbert Calkins, but decided to hold his tongue. The fewer the people who knew his business, the better. That was a maxim he'd stuck close to for a long time and it hadn't really failed him yet, so why rock that particular boat? Mose, though he knew him only as long as he'd been in town, was as honest and as tight-lipped as the day was long—or in the case of midwinter days, short. But eminently trustworthy.

Slocum headed over to the back of the store where clothing was kept. His own sheepskin-lined winter coat was still in good condition, but he sorely needed wool socks, a couple of new pairs of woolen longhandles, a wool head scarf, a knitted cap, and lined hide mittens, if they had them. He'd prefer to make them, but he didn't have the luxury of time holed up in front of a roaring blaze in a mountain cabin all winter, much as that idea appealed to him.

Within minutes he was pleased to have found the necessary items, plus two new shirts and two wool blankets, and piled them on the counter. He rested a hand on the topmost blanket. "I wonder if I could get this order delivered to Moses's livery?"

The old shopkeep, a large man with spectacles perched on the end of a bulbous veined nose, looked at the stack and, after a quick mental tally, realized the order was more than large enough to warrant sending an errand boy to the livery with a handcart. "Surely. I can have it down there within the hour. Anything else you want, just pile it up on the counter, then I'll tally it up."

"I appreciate that. I think I'm just about all set. Oh, except for three bottles of bonded whiskey and fifty cents' worth of the hard candy that tastes like fruit, those colored ones in the end jar."

"Got it."

"Great. That should do it."

The merchant made a list of all the goods piled on the counter, with their prices, his lips moving softly the entire time in silent calculation.

"I don't suppose you happen to have any snowshoes, do you?"

The old man paused, marked his place on the list with a thumb—here was a man used to being interrupted, thought Slocum—and glanced toward the rafters, poking his pencil skyward. "Got them, but they're not new by any shake. Let you have 'em for . . . two dollars."

Slocum looked up at the pair of beavertail shoes hanging just out of reach. "May I take a look at them?"

"Surely." The merchant lifted them down with a long, hooked pole and deposited them in Slocum's arms. Snowshoes were another item he would have liked to have made for himself. He'd done so once years before and had been pleased both with the work and with the results. But this pair seemed quite serviceable; the rawhide lacing was not brittle but looked as though it could use some bear grease conditioning. And the wood was in fine shape, not cracked on the steam-bent curves. The leather boot harnesses were dried, but looked as if he could revive them—nothing he couldn't fix during a night or two around a campfire.

The old merchant poked them with the tip of his pencil. "I'll send along a small jar of grease to bring the leather and rawhide back to prime. How's that sound?"

Slocum nodded. "Sounds good to me. I'll take them, thanks."

While he waited for the man to tally up the final account, he nibbled a cracker and warmed his hands by the stove in the middle of the room. From behind him, the merchant said, "Do me a favor and toss in another piece of wood. My old bones don't like the cold. Seems to me you're taking to the trail. Better you than me. I go anywhere, it's going to be south. But that ain't likely. At any rate you're better equipped for the cold than that goober who passed through here a couple of days back."

"Oh?" said Slocum. He closed the stove and turned back to the counter.

"Yep, a dandy sort, said he was headed northwest. Wouldn't take no advice about what to buy. Ended up with things only a fool would bring on the trail. And no pack animal, to boot. I expect if you are headed in the same direction, you'll find his greenhorn carcass stiff as a tree root and half as pretty."

"Do you recall what he looked like?"

"Sure do—here's your tally, by the way." He slid the list to Slocum and tapped a circled figure at the bottom.

Slocum winced inside, but figured for the pile of goods it was fair. Lucky thing Ginny Garfield wasn't concerned about money.

"That fella had oiled, wavy gold hair and a waxed mustache to match. I bet he's one of them types to spend time before a looking glass of a morning." The merchant shook his head. "And the clothes he wore, too fancy by half. But he was nothing if not confident. Then again, he came in here on one of those days when it was above freezing, so he was bound to think the best, as we all tend to do on such days. I tried to talk him out of leaving, told him the train would be along, but he laughed, said it wasn't going where he needed to be."

"Did he say where that was?" Slocum hoped for an answer as he handed over his cash.

The old man took the money, counted it, and shook his head. "Nope, never did say. Just that it was northwestward. Oh, and he did say something about mountains, but that'd be about all he did say. So after that, your guess is as good as mine." He looked at Slocum over his spectacle rims, as if awaiting an explanation for the questioning Slocum had given him.

But Slocum knew he'd heard all that the man had to offer. He thanked him and headed back to the hotel for a last chat with Ginny.

Mountains? he thought as he walked. What could a city man like Delbert Calkins want that far to the west? Unless he didn't start out as a city man at all. Maybe there's more to the fellow than any of the Garfields—or anyone else but Calkins himself—knows. Or else the man might have known he was being tailed and decided to plant a few false clues as to his intended direction.

That would make following him more difficult. If he had to bet, Slocum thought Calkins was going to head southward before long. Maybe he already had. The very thought of it made his gut tighten—the sooner he got on the trail, the better he'd feel.

"Only one way to find out," said Slocum, mounting the steps of the Hoyt House for what he suspected was the last time. He intended to walk on by the front desk and head up the stairs, but a sharp "Ahem" paused him. He turned to see the fat man from the night before. This time he wasn't smiling.

"May I help you, sir?"

Slocum smiled. "Yep, you can go back to what you were

doing. I'm heading upstairs to see Miss Garfield, then I'm gone."

"Really, sir. This is a house of fine accommodation, I don't think it's seemly for someone such as"—he looked Slocum up and down, then back to his face—"such as yourself to be traipsing in and out as if you were a guest."

"Well now," said Slocum, scratching his stubbled chin. "It's true I have been in and out a bit, but I am a guest of a guest and I happen to know she's what you might consider a top guest, am I right?"

Already the fat man's face was popping a sweat and uncertainty peppered his brow.

Slocum didn't wait for a response. "That's what I thought. Now, shall I tell the good lady that someone such as"—he looked the fat man up and down slowly—"such as yourself wishes to see her about a . . . problem?"

"No sir, that won't be necessary. A case of mistaken identity, as it turns out." He offered a flaccid smile and went back to pretending he was busy with a ledger book.

Slocum sighed and headed on upstairs.

5

As he promised, he was back at Mose's place before an hour had passed. The old man had indeed sold him a solid-looking packhorse that Slocum insisted on paying half again more for than what the old man was asking.

Then the goods from the mercantile arrived, and after Slocum tipped the delivery boy, he and Mose laid everything out on the floor of the barn, repacked it all, arranging it on the pack saddle that Mose threw in with the sale of the horse. Working with Mose was a pleasure and Slocum knew he would miss the man's company.

He also knew Mose was particularly fond of a certain type of brandy and little black cigars that one bar along a side street sold. So after he'd left Ginny Garfield at the hotel, Slocum had taken a detour and bought Mose a couple of bottles of brandy and a tin full of the little cigars.

And then it seemed all of a sudden he was packed, the horses loaded, and the gear secured well. His good-byes had been said to Mose and Ginny Garfield. Despite the logic of the case and his urge to be in the wild and free of town life once more, Slocum felt a knot of nervousness in his gut for leaving on such a chase in winter, and after a man he'd not seen, nor been personally slighted by.

But he knew deep down that the reason he agreed to take on the job was in part because the girl was so persuasive, and in part because he knew what it was like to lose a family member. He also knew he just had to get out of the town and back on the trail and on his own. Even if it meant doing so in the middle of the winter. He relished the peculiar demands that winter would put on him on the trail, just to stay alive, let alone find the devil he'd soon be chasing.

"Talk about a cold trail," he said as he passed the last building on the western edge of town. Before him stretched a long, undulating plain for as far as he could see, dotted with a gradually lessening number of buildings. But he was right, it felt damn good to be back on the move, even with the slicing wind that kicked up almost as soon as he left town behind.

He was pleased with his purchases and had taken a few moments to don new woolen underclothes, fresh socks, mittens, and a neck scarf. The horses both seemed pleased, too, to have a purpose and stepped lively along. There would be ample sign of the man's direction, Slocum hoped, with no notion that anyone might follow him. He hoped that meant the man would be unobservant and perhaps even careless in covering his trail. He also hoped the man stopped off in a town to do some gambling. It might be far too much to hope for that the man would decide to stay on for a week in this made-up town in Slocum's mind. But all that hoping sure would make Slocum's life so much easier.

"If wishes were horses," he said to the Appaloosa, turning his head briefly to check on the packhorse, "then beggars would ride."

6

"Why don't you act like you're supposed to, horse?"

Delbert Calkins hammered his heels hard into the horse's ribs, but the big brute didn't have the gumption to speed up. He didn't understand it. The damned animal started the trip just fine, but had been getting slower and more ornery every day they got farther from Bismarck.

No, this horse didn't make sense. He'd fed it snow, so he knew it was getting water, and the man he'd won the horse from back in Bismarck had said it wouldn't need much more than a couple of handfuls of oats a day to keep it going, at least until he reached the next town.

But it had been, as near as he could remember, five days and he hadn't seen a single other horse or rider, and certainly no houses. And a town? Forget it. At this rate, they'd both freeze or starve to death—or both. Still, Delbert felt sure that he had made the right choice in spreading the news around town that he was headed northwest. Anybody that damn Ginny Garfield might set on his trail would think twice about heading north in the winter. He figured he'd leave town headed in that direction, give it a few days, make it look good, then cut south, ramble along until it got warmer, then cut east again.

55

He hadn't really spent much time on horseback before, not more than a few minutes here and there. But he figured that being a Chicago boy, and surviving in the hard city, he should have little trouble out here, where the worst thing that could happen was that you'd run into a stray Indian. And since he was a good shot with his revolver and with his derringer, savages were the least of his worries.

At least that was how he'd been thinking when he left Bismarck. He tried to make it look like he'd be outfitted for cold weather, but that nosy old man at the mercantile kept pestering him about more gear and buying a packhorse and filling it with goods.

Delbert smirked and shook his head. Sure the man would say that—he was in the business of selling all those very things he wanted Delbert to buy!

"Did he think I was born yesterday?" He shook his head and jammed his heels into the horse's gut again. The beast picked up its pace for a half-dozen steps, then settled back into its hangdog walk.

He hated to admit it, but he was beginning to worry for his life. He also didn't dare veer from the trail he'd been following. If he did, and he turned south instead, he might not come across any civilization. But, he rationalized, if he stuck with this road, at least to the next settlement—no matter how small—he was sure to get warm, buy more supplies, maybe trade in this horse for something not so skinny and slow. Then he'd head south, by God. And leave all this cold and snow behind. He'd also kill for a cup of coffee. Oh, how he missed hot coffee and warm food.

Two hours later, as if in answer to his murmured prayers, Delbert saw something on the horizon that could well have been a log. Still, it was something to head toward, something that looked different than the long, flat white plain. And the closer he and the horse walked, the more he began to see that it was maybe a house. Or at least some long, low structure. And then he saw a thin wisp of smoke rising up from what must have been a chimney. Warmth!

No amount of pleading or dragging could induce the horse to move faster, so it took them another thirty minutes to reach the long, low building. It sat before him, half-covered in snow and reeking of decay and smells the likes of which Delbert had never experienced, even in Chicago.

He led the horse slowly across the hard-frozen river, their footsteps not sliding but crunching in the stiff, granulated surface. As they emerged up the far bank, he saw the dark bulky shape of a person tending a couple of sorry-looking horses in a small corral to the right of the building. He led the horse in that direction, and when it came within sight of the others, it perked its ears forward and sniffed, then sped up, pushing past him. He let go of the reins.

It wasn't until the beast had nosed into the paltry bit of yellowed hay in the rack that the person noticed he was not alone. And it wasn't until the person yelped that Delbert realized the bulky shape was not a he, but a woman. She stared at the strange horse for a moment, then spun around, saw Delbert, and backed up, wide-eyed, shaking her head.

Delbert noticed several things about her all at once. She was built like a barrel, she was probably not yet thirty, she had dark hair and skin the color of tobacco, and she had been beaten about the face quite recently. Her lips were both split, one eyelid was puffed and slitted, within which her eye roved and struggled to see.

"Hello there," said Delbert, walking forward and extending a hand. "I am Delbert. I wonder if I might purchase some feed for my horse . . ." It was then that he really noticed the sorry state her horses were in. The two of them stood still, barely fluttering open their eyelids. They shook, either from the cold wind or malnourishment, he wasn't sure. But judging from their thin state, he was surprised they were still alive. Beyond them, he saw the bone-jutted hides of what looked like another one or two horses, dead and partially covered in drifted snow.

"You leave here now," said the girl.

Delbert was surprised at how low and strong her voice was.

"You take me with you."

"What? No, no, I plan on going in there for a bit of a warm-up. That is, if you don't mind me inviting myself into your home. I am tired and can pay you for whatever food you may have on hand." As he said it, he looked around, noting there wasn't much in the way of anything. Except what looked like a pile of picked-over bones beside the door.

"They"—she jerked her chin at the sod-covered hut—"will kill you if you go in there. Take me with you." She reached into the filthy folds of the layers of cloth she wore.

Delbert immediately drew back, unbuttoned his own coat, and rested a hand on the butt of his pistol.

She didn't notice, and instead pulled out not a weapon but a small pouch. "I pay you to take me from here."

The sight of the little leather sack made Delbert Calkins pause. He ran his tongue tip over his bottom lip and smoothed his long mustaches, ending with a slight twirling of the tips. The sack looked like it had weight to it—maybe this Indian woman had some bit of gold? Dusky jewels unknown to white men? He had to know. Delbert reached for the sack.

The woman pulled it away, smiling. It was not a pretty smile. Most of her teeth were missing, and those that remained were shadowed and pitted. "You take me with you?"

Her words snapped Delbert from his gem-induced reverie. "Yes, yes, of course. But tell me . . . ma'am." He smiled a little off-kilter and raised one eyebrow, the look the ladies all seemed to like. "Just how do you expect to go with me? My horse, admittedly in much better shape than those—no offense—is not up to hauling me and"—he looked her up and down—"you around on his old swayed back."

Her face fell. She looked behind her to the leaning racks of bone once known as horses. They barely moved an eyelid; breath lightly rose from their nostrils. She looked down at her feet, crushed.

"Tell you what," said Delbert. "I don't have enough money to go buy you a horse, but if you are willing to lend me your purse there, I will ride off and buy one for you."

She smiled again, her battered eyes bright. "Yes?"

He nodded. "Yes."

"Where you do this?"

"You tell me. Which way should I head to find a suitable horse for you? Then I will purchase said beast, bring it back here, and take you away from this pit of treachery."

She still smiled. "That way," she said, pointing beyond the chimney. It was to the left of the direction he'd come.

"Are you certain I will find . . . a horse seller in that direction?"

She nodded, still smiling.

He smiled back and held out his hand. She gladly, willingly placed its promising weight in his palm. He hefted it once, liked what he felt, and decided not to insult the woman by inspecting its contents just then. Later, on the trail, he would see what its depths offered.

From within the low building came a shout. The words were unintelligible to Delbert, but they nonetheless jerked the woman's head around, instant terror seizing her features. She had obviously been summoned.

"I should go now," said Delbert, nodding to her. "And so should you. I will be back in all haste. Trust me!" He offered her a half bow and mounted up on his horse. He also kept his coat open, just in case whatever creature had howled from the guts of that building decided to confront him before he could make an escape from this hellish place.

The squat Indian woman hustled to the house. Halfway there, she stopped, looked at him, and said, "You come back for me."

He nodded solemnly to her. "You have my word on it, ma'am. I shall return."

He watched her continue the last few yards to the building, then scurry around it. Soon he heard a door squawk open and, with what sounded like much effort, clunk shut. More thick shouts erupted from inside, coupled with dog barks and sharp sounds, then crying. It had to be the woman. Delbert shook his head as he tugged on the reins. The horse still mouthed down the coarse yellow hay. "Poor thing," said Delbert. "But she does make terrible choices in what men to trust, doesn't she?"

The horse jerked its head back to the hay. Delbert let it grab another mouthful as he pondered which way to go. He didn't trust the woman's judgment for an instant. Anyone who let herself be so abused and duped was not right in the head.

The nasty dugout was built along the river. And rivers ran south, if he remembered correctly, so he should just follow it. Problem was, he didn't know what way it flowed—the entire thing was iced over. He looked at the meandering path it cut through the flat, snowdrifted landscape, but it didn't help. What trees there were looked no taller than man height, but they leaned every which way, instead of all in one direction, say, toward the south.

In the end, he decided to continue on in the direction he'd been heading, feeling in his bones that somehow it would lead him southward. Yes, he was sure of it. He smiled as he led his horse on out of that place, leaving it behind.

Surely he would come to a town soon.

7

Slocum had been riding for the better part of four days when he came to a dugout soddy hard by the frozen banks of the Chilawaw River. Even from a distance it didn't look like the sort of place where he wanted to spend much time. He still had plenty in the way of supplies and he didn't particularly want the company of a handful of drunk hiders stinking up the place and belching and farting like old plow horses, then laughing at the cheap amusement. But what he did want was information. He had little more than hunch to go on that Delbert Calkins had headed in this very direction.

He figured he could choke down a glass of whatever godawful popskull the proprietor distilled if it meant confirming his hunch about Calkins. As he drew nearer to the place, he saw a half-dozen ravens circling what he assumed was the corral, since the loose collection of leaning rails seemed to keep the horses in and nothing else out.

At the first sign of their approach, the two horses in the corral nickered and raised their heads from a snow-filled trough. He saw a few wispy remnants of yellowed hay. Beyond the leaning corral and thin horses standing hip-shot, their hind ends to the wind, Slocum spied the partially drifted over remains of two more horses, their hides so sunken they looked to have starved to death. They also appeared to have been hacked into for meat—either by men or scavengers. Probably one and the same at this place, he guessed.

Slocum decided he'd keep his animals cinched tight together and keep himself close to the door once he got inside. He also decided he'd make this a short stop.

He rode over to the long side of the building, the only place he saw with any type of entrance into the structure. It was also laid out such that it caught the full brunt of the prevailing wind. He shook his head as he dismounted.

Surely when they built the long, low eyesore, the builders would have known which way the wind blew and so should have positioned the building accordingly to avoid it. People were thick in the head, by and large. They meant well, but frequently they puzzled him. Rich, poor, young, old, people were frequently more of a menace to themselves than the natural world could ever be.

He wrapped the reins around the checked, weathered hitch rail, lifted the flap of the rifle boot, and slid out the Winchester. It would not do to lose it to someone who might be skulking around the corner. But mostly, he thought as he cradled it, he wanted it along inside in case things got surly. He'd been to enough of these soddy trading posts to know how unruly the inhabitants could be. He double-checked that his packhorse was secured well to the Appaloosa and headed to the door.

The edge of the roof was low enough that it came to his chest. To each side of the door, the snow was littered with stove ashes, broken crockery, vomit, and yellow circles drilled into the snow. Just to the right of the door sat a pile of bones that looked as if they'd been gnawed by wolves.

Slocum reminded himself to skip the stew if it was offered. Bending low, he reached for the strap leather handle, thought better of it, and stood as much to the side of the door as he could, given the trash dumped there.

As soon as he rapped on the door, a loud vicious-sounding barking began. One dog, big from the sounds of it, and then it must have lunged at the door because he heard it slamming into the cobby planking.

Almost as soon as the barking began, a man's voice bellowed for it to shut the hell up. Something heavy slammed into the door just after the dog, then something else must have been thrown, because the next sound Slocum heard was the dog yowling in pain.

Slocum unbuttoned his coat and slipped the edge of it behind his left holster.

The door swung inward, dragging across its own grooves on a rough-log floor. Piggy eyes set in a welter of grime and hair stared at Slocum. "What you want?"

Slocum peered back at a big, bearded face. "Sign said this is a trading post."

"Yeah, so?"

"You open for business?"

The man's little eyes squinted, then the door swung wider. The rest of him was as big as his head was hairy. A wave of close air, unwashed men, and meat gone off rolled at Slocum.

"Well," said the fat man. "Come on in. You're lettin' the warm out."

Slocum pulled in a last gasp of cool, fresh air, bent low, and stepped on into the dark space. "The dog going to cause me worry?"

"Nah. I fixed him up."

As Slocum looked around the dark space, he didn't move from the door, just enough to let the man close it. His eyes took too damn long to adjust to the dark, smelly room, but were aided by a lone window in the far end that managed to let a thin slant of light into the dank space. Part of it was jagged glass, the rest thin-skinned hide. A nearby gap in the wall was stuffed with rags.

Just under the ragged window sat two hulking forms

covered in buffalo coats. Hiders—they would account for some of the stink. The only thing worse than the stink of death trailing a buffalo skinner was the stink of two of them together in a close space. Naturally they were backed up to the stove.

The fat owner didn't seem to mind the stink in the least. In fact, thought Slocum, they all looked like they'd shared the same ma. He finally located the dog, a long-legged mongrel with patchy hair and a mottled coat. He looked blind in one eye but the other, a black unblinking orb, regarded every move Slocum made. A menacing growl, steady and low, crawled up from deep in the dog's throat.

"He won't bother you none. Not unless you get it in your head to cause me a headache." The fat man cut his eyes toward the two hiders, who obliged with weak chuckles, then turned their attention back to the nearly empty cloudy bottle between them on the small table. Slocum noticed a third glass and chair.

"Wouldn't think of it," said Slocum, scanning the room. He noted another door behind the bulk of the barman. "Where did your other drinking buddy go?" He nodded toward the table.

"Oh," said the barman. "That's my glass. We was . . . playing cards when you banged on the door."

Slocum didn't see any cards on the table.

"What do you want anyway?"

"I was passing, on my way west, thought I'd stop. I'm looking for a man—"

"You one of them types?"

Slocum ignored this and continued. "He's blond, waxed mustache, dressed like a dandy, doesn't seem to be experienced with winter travel."

"Mister, you gonna buy something or flap your gums?" The fat man wiped his face with his apron, a begrimed affair that Slocum was sure hadn't been off his body, let alone washed, in years.

"Got any cigars?" he said, half joking.

"Ceegars? What in hell do we look like, mister? Some hoity-toity fancies to you?" The big, begrimed man dragged the corner of the filthy apron across his bearded face and only succeeded in rearranging the runnels of tobacco spittle glistening in his beard.

"Whiskey, then," said Slocum.

"All I got's corn liquor."

"That'll do. How much?"

"Since you're askin', it's a dollar."

"Kind of steep, isn't it?" Slocum pulled a coin out of an inner coat pocket. He made it a rule to keep coins in various pockets so he wouldn't have to pull out a laden coin purse or wad of cash—not that he had to worry about that all that often.

The barman poured the booze from a crock into a squat, green glass that looked to have been licked and dipped in a gut pile. Slocum picked up the glass with two fingers and did his best to hold it up to the light. "Got a clean glass?"

"That's as good as it gets." The man stood waiting for Slocum to drink.

"I'm not so sure I need a drink that bad."

"You got to drink it now. I done poured it."

"How about you tell me if the man I described came through here recently, and if I like what I hear, I'll leave the dollar and the liquor. You can have both."

"And if you don't like what you hear?" The fat man behind the plank bar stared at him.

"Then you'll keep talking until I hear something useful."

One of the hiders set his own glass down and said, "Must be you're getting money to find that man."

For the size of man he was, Slocum reckoned his voice should be lower. He'd be embarrassed if such a sound came out of his mouth.

The hider stood, pushing his chair back along the rough floor. "Could be you got that money on you."

Slocum tensed, kept his back to the closed door, and tried

to keep the dog and the three men all in view. He was nearly successful. The dog began slowly walking toward the door.

"Do you really think I'd get paid before I found him?"

This slowed down the men, seemed to challenge their thinking.

The barman said, "Could be I heard tell of a fella like that come through a few days back."

Excellent, thought Slocum. My first solid lead letting me know Delbert Calkins had been there. "I don't suppose you have any useful memories of his visit, do you?"

"You got to buy something more in order to let you know what I know about the man."

The big hider took another step toward the door behind Slocum. Slocum uncradled the Winchester. "Hold on there, big boy."

The man paused. "What? Can't a man take a piss?"

"Yep, he can. Judging from the smells in here, I'd guess you wouldn't be the first."

"I aim to head outside, mister."

Slocum thumbed back the hammer on the rifle. "Then we'll both go."

"I knowed you were odd," said the fat man behind the counter, slamming his hands on the bartop. An empty bottle jumped, fell over, and rolled off the planks.

This chatter was getting him nowhere, and if it continued much longer, he would suspect they had someone outside working on relieving him of his horses and goods.

"I'll bid you good day, then, gentlemen." He didn't think he'd get any more out of them.

"Now hold on a minute, mister. You . . ." the barman looked almost desperate to keep him in there. "You ain't finished your drink."

"Ain't started it yet either." He reached behind him for the leather strap door handle when, on a nod from the barman, the big man to his left lunged at him. At the same time the dog launched into a dive straight.

Slocum figured the dog was a faster mover, and though he hated to do it, he pivoted enough on his left leg that he was able to kick the airborne beast in the throat. It made a gagging sound and crashed into the rough wall behind it. He had no time to see if the kick had been enough to keep the dog down for a few seconds, for the great bull of a man was almost on him. Slocum raised the rifle and managed to jam the snout of it hard against the big hider's forehead. He saw the skin pucker as the man's head drove into the barrel end.

The hider stopped in his tracks, almost teetering on his mammoth legs as Slocum thumbed the hammer back the rest of the way. By then he heard the dog coming to, sucking breath through its damaged windpipe, but it didn't sound good. Slocum hoped he hadn't dealt the dog a mortal blow. He reckoned he'd find out soon enough.

He had to get on out of there before whoever it was who'd headed out when he headed in made off with his horses and gear. But the two other men were advancing.

Beyond the smelly hider who Slocum was propping up with the snout of his rifle, he heard the other one wheezing into action. He glanced quickly over the closer man's shoulder, and when he did, he heard the godawful sound of two hammers thumbing back on a double-barrel shotgun. He looked back in time to see the barman level off on him. Slocum could almost feel the barman's fat fingers tense on the triggers.

From directly behind, the cur, while not fully recovered, was drawing breath enough to begin another angry lunge. Slocum knew they had no reason to keep him alive. They had his gear and horses outside and whatever they could scavenge off his dead body. Me or them, he said to himself, and dropped low, then dove to his left.

The hulking hider lurched into the space Slocum had been just as the barman squeezed the shotgun's triggers.

The double booms filled the room with thunder that rattled Slocum's teeth and clouded the air with smoke. Sod chunks, rock, and snow rained downward. His right leg was pinned, he assumed under the fat hider, but it was unmoving weight. He clawed free a Colt Navy and swung it upward just as the second hider regained his senses and, yelling, lunged at Slocum.

The Colt sent a bullet straight into the center of the fat man's mustache, cleaving his face right under the nose. The back of the man's head blossomed outward, spraying the haggard window a dripping red even as he pitched forward. Slocum rolled as far as he could to the side, but his leg remained pinned. Then he remembered the dog—where was that damn beast?

From the bar, he heard the *thunk-thunk* of shells ejecting and he knew the barman was thumbing in two more. The ringing in his ears didn't hide the raw rage of the barman. He was howling, and then Slocum saw why. The first two blasts had dropped the big hider *and* the dog. Both lay on the floor where Slocum had been standing before the door—the dog half sprawled on the big buffalo-hide-clad form, both a hairy, matted mess of blood, twitching and whimpering.

It was dark at the floor and Slocum knew he had but a couple of seconds before the big barman would locate him. That's all he would need. He swung the rifle and pistol both into play a fraction of a second before the barman did so with the shotgun.

From the ground, and pinned as he was, Slocum's aim was off, as he knew it might be. But his twin bullets caught the man high in the greasy apron, the second in the chin. The barman's scream rattled into a gag, and just before he collapsed on top of the makeshift plank-and-barrel bartop, his reflexes touched off both of his gun barrels.

Slocum hugged the grimy floor, pressed himself as flat as possible as the shots blasted at the walls and low ceiling. More deafness, rattling teeth, and hunks of the soddy structure raining down on him. He needed a few minutes to wait out the smoke, but he knew that every second he spent in there among the dead and dying was another second someone was making off with his horses and gear.

He used the Winchester's butt to push against the still twitching fat man pinning his leg. A gurgle of pain rose from under the buffalo coat. "Sorry, buddy," said Slocum, but he kept shoving.

Just when he thought he was going to have to scrabble in the smoke and dirt and near dark for something else to help pry the big bastard off him, the body gave enough that he slipped his leg free from under the bleeding mess. He almost lost his boot as he slid it out, but managed to keep his toes curled, and out came the boot, too.

He staggered to his feet, then saw the door he'd come in was blocked by the dying man's body. His head had slammed into the thing. There was no way Slocum was going to budge the brute. In the jostling he'd given the man in trying to free his leg, the dog had slid from atop the man and clunked to the floor.

The smoke had cleared enough that Slocum knew the two men he'd shot were dead, saw no movement from either. But the dog and the hider who'd received the shotgun blasts were both still alive. The dog's tongue lolled out of its mouth, and its eyelids twitched.

The stink of hot blood steaming in the already fetid quarters almost made Slocum gag, but he had to end the dog's suffering before he could bolt out the back door. "Sorry, chum. May your next run be a better one." He shot the dog in the head with his Colt and the beast stilled. The man beneath still spasmed and a thin wheeze rose from him.

Slocum wasn't sure if that was the man's last gasp or if he'd farted. He winced at what he had to do, but knew there was no way the man would live much longer. He thumbed back the hammer once more, toed the man with his boot as a last check, and felt the peculiar unresponsive feeling only a dead body can offer.

"Good," said Slocum, moving toward the back door. He had to move the legs of the dead barman, since they were also blocking the door, but he managed to clear them away enough to yank open the door.

Fresh, cold air flowed in, and never had anything tasted, felt, or smelled so good. He yanked harder and pushed his way though. Immediately, even though his eyes recoiled at the light stabbing them, he scanned the long plain beyond the back of the soddy. He saw nothing. He dragged his leg through the narrow door gap and stood outside, relishing the full, deep breaths he pulled in.

He coughed, spat, and ran around the right end of the hovel. There were the three bonerack horses, clustered at the far end of the leaning corral. They looked a lot worse than he had first noticed—open sores, and so thin it seemed as if their bones would poke through their hides in a hundred spots. He thumbed back the hammer of the Colt and made his way around to the front.

Just as he'd expected, his Appaloosa and packhorse were gone. He saw the tracks, smaller than a fourth fat man would make, but someone had made off with them for sure. He ran along the full front of the building, and there, heading southward away from the left end of the building, someone was astride the Appaloosa and kicking and flailing for all he was worth. Whoever the someone was, they weren't much of a rider, though Slocum was sure the Appaloosa wasn't helping matters much.

A horse thief is a horse thief, and I am sunk if I lose my horses and gear out here. He was thankful that whoever it was hadn't gotten as far as someone with riding experience would have. He lay down in the snow, prone, levered a shell, cocked the hammer of the rifle, and pulled in a deep breath. He sighted on the broad black-clad back of the retreating form— then shifted his aim slightly in hopes of hitting a shoulder instead of the middle of the back. He'd done enough killing for today.

He let the breath half out and fired. He didn't wait to see a reaction. At that distance, he wasn't too sure his shot would do anything more than piss off the thief.

He cranked another round in and was about to repeat the procedure when the black coat whipped sideways and flopped off the horse's back.

"Now that's more like it," he said, standing up and wincing at the dull pain in the leg the fat man had fallen on.

He kept his eyes on the horses and they did slow, but only because the rider's left leg was tangled in the stirrup. He considered retrieving one of the horses in the corral, but rejected the thought immediately. They wouldn't carry him ten feet without wheezing. Instead, he took off at a lope through the hard, crusted snow straight across the sunned, snowy span toward the slowly retreating figures. The throbbing in his leg worked out with each long step he took. Soon he saw the Appaloosa turn, as he had hoped it would.

Slocum noted with dismay that the rider must be dead, or damn near so, because he saw the man's head whapping against the horse's legs near the ground. His shoulders and arms rose and fell hard with each erratic step the Appy took.

He bet himself a double shot of bourbon that the horse would tire of this flopping mess that it couldn't seem to get shed of. Question was, would it take off at a hard run in an attempt to dislodge it, or just stop altogether? He hoped for the latter. And soon a smile began to pull wide on his stubbled face.

The horse was stopping, and with it the packhorse. Now he just had to make damn sure as he approached that they wouldn't bolt when they caught sight of him. To the horses he would appear to be another in a long series of threats and annoyances, and he knew the Appaloosa had probably reached its tolerance limit for the day.

Slocum kept up his loping run until he drew within fifty yards of the huffing beasts, their breath pluming in the chill afternoon air. Nothing that he could see rose from the flopped form still hanging from the left stirrup. The Appaloosa pranced in annoyance and Slocum winced when he saw the horse step down hard on the thrashed rider's arm. Damn, he thought, that had to hurt. If the man were alive, he would surely have reacted.

As he drew closer, Slocum saw the battered form, blood and snow ground together into the patched, black wool coat. The head was hatless and a thatch of dark hair ended his hopes that it might be Delbert Calkins. No such luck. Still, he felt bad for not being able to take the thief alive. But then what would he do with him? He was days from anywhere he might drop off the bastard, let alone finding any law. He guessed he was well into Canada anyway. No worry about it now. The rider he'd shot was looking dead from this distance.

"Whoa, boy. Easy now, easy," Slocum kept up a steady, calming patter, or what he hoped was calming, to appease the nerved-up stepping of the Appaloosa. It worked, and when he reached the packhorse, which, as old Mose had promised, proved to be a steady creature of even character, the beast barely trembled. He ran a reassuring hand along its rump, up along the load, noting it was still secured well.

When he reached the horse's head, he grabbed the lead line and ran his hand along it to the Appaloosa. The big horse, as he'd expected, danced. Slocum had to look down again at the pulped mess that was the man he'd shot. And he got the biggest shock of his surprise-filled day: The shot man was a stout, dark-skinned woman, Indian most likely, as sadly evidenced by the flayed open coat and shirt, a bare breast exposed and speckled with blood.

"Oh hell," he said, looking at the battered face and pulped limbs in the blood-and-snow-pocked black wool coat.

He ground-tied the Appaloosa and laid the rifle down just away from it. Then he grabbed hold of the stirruped boot of the unfortunate thief and wrestled it through the wood-and-leather stirrup. The leg flopped free and he dragged the body away from the horse a few feet. He glanced down at the poor woman and bent to cover her exposed breast. Her shirt was a ragged mess, but he managed to pull the coat tightly around her. And as he bent low over her, he noticed a faint puff of breath rise from her mouth into the frigid air.

"Oh God," he whispered. As if he didn't feel bad enough. "Hey?" he whispered. "Hey, ma'am?"

All manner of emotion rushed at him and he fought to quell it as he reached toward her battered face. Her eyelids fluttered at his touch.

"What the hell have I done?" he whispered.

"Aaaah," said the woman. "I . . ."

Slocum leaned close and put his ear to her face.

"I . . . should have killed them myself."

"Who?" said Slocum.

"Bastards . . . hiders . . ."

"They hurt you?"

The trace of a smile appeared on her face. "You save . . . me," she said. "Thank you."

It was like a punch to the gut. How could this have all gone so wrong? He exhaled and stared at her fluttering eyes. It looked like she was trying to open them, but losing the struggle. He figured he couldn't feel much worse, so he pressed his luck while he could, knowing she wasn't far from leaving this life altogether. "Ma'am . . . a blond man, golden hair, nice clothes, mustache . . . did you see him just a week ago?"

"Yes, he took my money . . ." she said, her eyelids still fluttering, then settling. He felt her head relax. "Such a pretty boy . . ."

And that was it. She sagged beneath his hand, and he felt the life leave her. Her head flopped to the side, and a last small breath drizzled out of her bloodied mouth.

Slocum sat like that for long minutes, until the cold seeped in under his coat. What could all this mean? Had she really seen Delbert? Where did she come from? Probably was sold to the barman for whiskey. Or stolen. He looked down at her as he laid her flat on the ground. With her eyes closed, her battered face seemed almost peaceful.

He regretted shooting her, but should he? Why hadn't he felt this way when he knew it was a man? Was he just becoming hardened to killing? He shook his head and stood, the cold making his sore leg stiff. This was no way to go about the job at hand. He had to bring this girl back to the trading post, try to find some way of identifying her. Maybe he could pass on the news of their deaths in the next town. What a mess you've made, Slocum. What a mess.

He slung the girl's lifeless, broken body over the Appaloosa's saddle, tied her there. The horse still fidgeted at the odd-feeling weight, but Slocum tugged the reins and they walked back to the low soddy.

Looking at it, he wished he'd never stopped. Wished he'd never agreed to tail this Delbert Calkins. He sighed. What's done is done, he almost said aloud, but even then he knew that the man had committed a crime, perhaps more than one, as such heartless characters generally did. And someone had to try to bring them to justice. If he didn't tail Calkins, that foolish innocent, Ginny Garfield, would end up robbed and worse in some stage-stop town on a cold trail in the middle of nowhere. Her job was staying where she should be—doting on her dithering rich father and considering how best to spend the fortunes that would eventually be left to her.

And besides, he could no more quell his urge to rove free than he could stop breathing. He had to keep moving. Like some sort of fish someone had once told him about. He forgot what it was, but when he heard that if it stopped moving it would die, he understood that immediately.

Slocum looked around, couldn't quite figure out what to do with the place, the bodies. If he left them all inside, it wouldn't be so bad, because they would freeze—at least for a while. Scavengers might show up, and if the place started stinking, they'd surely find their way in through the partially blasted-out roof and walls.

He toyed with burning the entire place with the bodies inside, as the ground was far too cold to dig in, but decided there was no way he could do that. It might end up looking like someone was trying to cover up a whole lot of killing. Well, wasn't that what it was? A whole lot of killing?

He sighed and dragged the girl's body off the saddle, carried her in through the back door. There was nothing for it. She hadn't wanted to be there, that much was certain, but he had no intention of leaving her out there on the plain for the wolves to get at.

It took him a few minutes, but Slocum managed to drag the sloppy carcasses of the two foul hiders and the barman down to the far end. He rested a hand on the small ramshackle stove and found it had nearly gone out. Good. The sooner the bodies cooled, the better.

Next he kicked aside the smashed remnants of the make-shift bar and laid the girl out. Beside her he laid the dog, who he bet had been like the girl, and had not wished for life among such savage men.

He wondered again how she had fallen in with them. Sold? Traded? Kidnapped? Didn't matter now, he told himself. For better or worse, she was now at peace. She had seemed pleased to have made it away from the clutches of the men. He stood over the girl and the dog for a moment, had no words to say, but hoped his thoughts might suffice.

When he left the dugout, he dragged the door shut hard behind him, wedged and angled poles from the corral before the doors. Then he turned his attention to the two horses, noting their labored breathing, the fact that they barely flinched when he went over to them.

Up close, he noted their sores had festered, weeping blood and pus. Their eyes were crusted over and their legs looked as if they pained them. He suspected they were frozen clear through, living skeletons too tough to know they were already dead. They were too far gone—there was no way he was going to be able to trail them behind his packhorse as he'd originally hoped.

He couldn't leave them to continue on as they were. What little feed there was consisted of an armload of foul yellowed chaff, more straw than hay, and of no value for eating. They would starve to death like the snow-covered racks of bones nearby, and then be savaged by wolves. Or worse, it might happen before they died.

He knew what he had to do. To each horse he apologized,

then shot them both in the temple. They staggered, dropped, and wheezed out their final breaths.

"Sorry," he said again. "Shouldn't have been this way." Then he mounted up on the Appaloosa, and leading the pack-horse, he rode away without once looking back.

Before he made it to the far western slope on the horizon, low, dark shapes appeared on the rise to the east of the trading post, from the direction he'd traveled. They were wolves and they were grateful for the stranger's leavings.

8

A week after leaving the trading post behind, Slocum still hadn't come upon a settlement. He reckoned he was getting damn close to the mountains, as swells in the landscape were becoming more numerous, as were an increasing number of ground-hugging bushes and small trees. He was pretty sure he was in Canada, but beyond that he had little notion if he was still on Calkins's trail or if he was just striking off on a long, fruitless quest.

Late in the day on what he guessed was a Friday, Slocum came upon a camp so suddenly it seemed as if it had appeared by magic. He had seen no sign of it, smelled no campfire, and yet there it was below in a small, snowed vale when he crested a rise. A thin old man in buckskins sat hunched before a decent cook fire, squinting into the full brunt of the smoke and sputtering about it. A few dozen yards away from the camp, a mule was doing its best to reduce a shrub to ground cover.

"Ho the camp!" said Slocum, reining up atop the rise.

The effect his words had on the old man was almost comical. The thin figure, red-eyed and snarling from the get-go, sprang to his feet, a skin hat askew on a head that Slocum guessed had very little hair on top, and a long beard parted and knotted at the end as if it were a thready gray napkin. The man's set of buckskins looked as if they'd spent time seasoning under a gut pile.

"What you want?" The old man's hands hovered near his waist, though to Slocum's eye he wasn't wearing any side arms. He did see a tomahawk and a big ol' skinning knife, both fringed and beaded with decoration. Slocum guessed the old-timer could probably part his hair with that Indian axe.

Slocum held up his hands. "I come in peace." He smiled. "Just want to know if you'd care to have a visitor for a spell."

The old man's eyes narrowed even more. "Depends on who the visitor is and how long he thinks a spell ought to be."

"Fair enough response. I'm the visitor, and as for a spell, that depends on how welcome I am. Could be anywhere from how long it takes to drink a cup of coffee to a night's rest before I move on in the morning."

The old man considered this, kept one hand by his tomahawk, while the other gnarled claw he ran through his beard thoughtfully. "Ain't got no coffee, so that's out."

"I have some."

With that, the old man's eyes widened and he almost smiled. "You do? Good beans?"

"Any beans are good when you don't have coffee."

Then the old man really did smile. Slapping a hand on his knee, he said, "Truer words weren't never spoken. Ride on down here and yarn out that coffee of yours. We'll flap our gums for a spell."

Slocum did just that, and within a few minutes, he had his horses picketed and had unpacked a sack of Arbuckle's. He passed it to the old man, who was practically salivating. "You mind if I stick my sniffer in that bag? It's been so long since I had anything but the memory of a cup of coffee that I figure I'd better ease into this experience, lest I explode from the commotion."

"Go right ahead, sir," said Slocum, not bothering to hide his smile. This could be a fun visit. He sensed the old-timer was harmless and lonely. And starved for coffee.

After the man had his good, long sniff, and they rested the tin pot on the rocks to boil, Slocum asked him just where he was.

The old man looked at him as if he'd asked him which way was hell. "By God, if ever there was a man who couldn't answer that, it's me. I'm Whiskey Pete, by the way. That's what they call me here and there and in another time. On account of I liked the stuff a little too much and it always got me in trouble. But I left all that behind. Nowadays, I just wander with Ethel, my mule over yonder." He nodded toward the hobbled beast browsing the bushes lining the camp.

"I don't ride her, though."

"No?" said Slocum, pouring two cups of strong, hot coffee.

"Nope, I just feel odd and queasy asking an animal to do something for me when I can do it pretty well myself." The old man made a funny sound with his nose. As he warmed to his subject, he leaned forward, using his hands to speak as much as his voice. "Why should that mule have to do its job and mine, too? I ask you."

He leaned back, as if awaiting an answer. Slocum was about to oblige when Pete leaned forward again. "I don't judge another man, you see. Can't do that without seeming like I'm full of beans. But I will offer my opinion."

"I can see that. Before you cogitate on it further, try this on for size." He handed the old man a tin cup brimming with aromatic coffee.

"Oh Lord, I almost forgot, what with all that palaver I was getting up to." His eyes glistened like a child with a penny standing before the candy counter. He closed them and sipped.

Slocum watched as the cup half disappeared into that ornate beard and pretty soon the man's eyes snapped wide.

"It is without doubt the best cup of coffee any man within a hundred miles of wherever it is we are has had. By God, but it's grand stuff is coffee."

Slocum sipped and nodded. "Yep, I will agree with you there."

"You lost or something?" Whiskey Pete looked at him over

the rim of his cup. It seemed he was going to keep it close by his mouth and nose for the entire time there was liquid in it.

"I don't believe so. That is to say, I don't exactly know where I'm headed, and I don't know where I am. I have a rough idea I'm in Canada and I know those peaks yonder"—he nodded westward—"are the Rockies."

The old man was too polite, Slocum noted, to ask just what it was that brought him all the way out there.

"'Bout the only thing I can tell you is yes, you're right—them are the Rockies. I been trailin' up and down 'em, one side or t'other, most of my adult life. And that's quite a spell. But whether we're in Canada or the States, I don't know, and I guess I don't rightly care much either way. Long as I'm aboveground and I still got my hair."

With that, he lifted his fur cap and revealed a gleaming dome of skin with nothing but a few wiry strands spiraling out of it here and there. He was smiling. "I'm all set."

"Sounds like a decent way to live. Mind if I ask how you get by?"

"Ask away. Nothing I like better than talking. And if it's talk about myself, then I like that even better!" He sipped his coffee again and said, "I trap, carve trinkets, trade goods with a Cree tribe up northwest of here." He half turned and waved a gnarled hand in the direction of snowy peaks far in the distance. "They winter and summer up there, in a pretty little valley alongside a river. Ain't been told to move yet by any whites, so I reckon they're still there. I'm considering heading that way before too long, maybe come spring. I got a sack full of carvings I figure might could get me some Indian food. I'm partial to the pemmican they make. Can't make it to save my ass, but them squaws, by God, they can make tasty pemmican."

"You don't recall seeing a stranger come through here recently, do you?"

With that the old man stiffened, his eyes lost their mirth, and he set the coffee cup down. "What makes you ask that?"

Tread lightly, Slocum told himself. He had obviously

touched on a nerve, so he decided to go for broke. "I'm tracking a man. He's believed to be a killer."

The old man once again positioned his arms such that it looked like he might let fly, even from his sitting position, with a tomahawk or knife—or both. "You the law?"

"Nope," said Slocum, shaking his head, careful to keep his hands in sight, on his coffee cup. "I am working privately for a family who were wronged by this man. I hired on to find him and bring him to justice."

"What's he look like, this stranger of yourn?"

"Truth be told, I've never seen him. But going by other people's descriptions, he's about my height, has blond hair and a waxed mustache—of which he is mighty impressed. He also dresses like a town man, a dandy gambler. I have reason to believe he's also not accustomed to travel on the trail, that he might be ill equipped."

The old man relaxed. "Well, I wish you was the law."

"Why's that?"

"Because that's the weasel bastard who cheated me out of my poke."

"What? Are you sure?" Slocum leaned forward, set down his cup.

The old man scratched his chin again. "Yep, yep," he said, nodding. "I may be old and spend too much time talking to my mule, but I'd say that's the very man. Course, except for the bit about being unaccustomed, as you say, to horse travel and trail life, I'd say he's the man. This fella was a dandy, sported finery such as you'll not see on the trail. And that mustache of his, well, he looked like one of them fellas who'd fall into a sty and come up smelling of rosewater. If you get my meaning."

Slocum nodded. "But you say he seemed trail hardened?"

"Yep," said the old man, helping himself to more coffee.

It was possible, of course, that Delbert had become accustomed to life on horseback in the time Slocum had been following him. But from what he'd been told, Calkins was a city man who'd left Bismarck needing supplies. "Which way was he headed, Pete?"

"Yonder, toward the mountains." His voice had taken on that dark tone again.

Clearly the stranger, if it had been Delbert Calkins, had wronged him mightily. To know he was still on the man's trail after all this time was a damn good feeling.

In the days after the mess at the trading post, he'd all but decided to head south along the mountains and send Miss Garfield the remainder of her money, tell her the trail had grown cold. But he knew her reaction—she'd take off after the man herself, and he couldn't let her come to such an end as that would surely bring.

"Can I ask how he cheated you?" Slocum knew this might be a sensitive topic, but he wanted whatever information he could gather.

"I invited him into my camp, much like I done with you—but you have the look of honesty about you. I guess I'd talked with Ethel a mite too long at that point—about a week past—and well, he pulled out a bottle of whiskey. And since we neither of us had coffee, and as it was colder than a gravedigger's backside, I allowed as how a drop or three of the stuff might help keep me from seizing up." He shook his head at the memory.

"Well, before I knew it, I was playing a shell game with him, right on that there blanket of mine." He nodded toward a worn striped Indian blanket rolled off to the side of the little camp. "Woke up to an empty poke."

He slipped a buckskin pouch out from under his shirt and danced it on his fingers. He wore it about his neck, but even without feeling it, Slocum could see that it was empty. "Not so much the few coins and nuggets I had that I minded losing, but there was a pretty blue rock in there give to me by a Navajo woman a long time past. I'll take it out of an evening and hold it and think of her." His rheumy eyes stared into the fire. "Good times, they was."

Slocum held his peace for a few moments, then said, "Did

you lose all that playing the game of chance with him, or did he just take it from you?"

"That's the thing, see . . . I don't know quite what happened. I told you that when me and whiskey meet up, one of us goes home with a sore head and a black eye. And it ain't never been any one of the two of us but me. Every time. So I guess I'll be man about it and say that I lost my goodies fair and square, gambling them away like that." He fell to musing again, staring at the flames. "All for a few swallows of popskull."

Slocum stood and stretched his back. "Well, I'll tell you, I have no interest in filching from you. But I am interested in anything else you might remember about the man. Like why he headed to the mountains. You said that Cree tribe winters there. I wonder what he'd want with them."

"Maybe nothing," said Pete, draining the pot as he poured himself another cup of coffee. He smiled. "That's the one good thing I can say come out of meeting up with that man. I never did get to tell him it seemed like he was headed the wrong way. Now that was a man who must have been lost."

Whiskey Pete had flecks of coffee grounds in his smoke-stained beard and in his teeth, but he looked to Slocum as if he was really enjoying every swallow of the thick stuff.

"Them Crees are hunters mostly," said the old man. "Far as I know they ain't got much that any white man—least what civilized whites I've met—would want. Me, I'm white as the day is long, but I tell you they got it all figured out, them Indians."

"How so?" said Slocum.

"Don't seem to want for anything, even when they don't have much. As long as they can fill their bellies, they seem to be happy. I envy that."

"Do they have Arbuckle's?"

Whiskey Pete leaned back, scratched his chin again. "Now you may have a point there. I reckon they are missing out on a little something." He yawned, saw Slocum was headed for his horse. "You ain't leaving just yet, are you?"

"No. That is, if you don't mind sharing your camp for the night. I'll be heading out first light."

"I'd welcome the company. I got some antelope steaks just right for a feed."

Slocum began unstrapping the packhorse's load, pulled free a sack of supplies, and brought it over to the old man. "That sounds perfect. In that bag you'll find flour, salt, beans—all manner of things that might help us come up with a first-class supper. I'll help you as soon as I strip the saddles and loads here. My horses are tuckered out."

But the old man probably didn't hear him—he was busy rummaging in the sack. With each item he pulled out, he licked his lips and grunted in approval. Then he looked over at Slocum. "You got enough to be sharing? I don't want to cut you short on your trip's supplies."

"Don't you worry about that," said Slocum. "I have plenty. And I'm grateful for the company. Now what say we make some biscuits to go with those steaks?"

"And maybe another pot of coffee?" The old man looked sheepish, but couldn't seem to stop himself from asking.

Slocum laughed. "Why not? Who needs sleep anyway?"

"Ha! Man after my own heart. Why, I remember the time . . ." The old man busied himself setting up the provisions and preparing the campfire, yammering the entire time about something that had happened to him years before. But Slocum was only half listening. His mind was on the route Delbert Calkins had taken. Why would he be heading toward the mountains? Could be he had gotten turned around somehow and truly was lost, as Whiskey Pete had guessed. But was Calkins really more knowledgeable about life on the trail than Slocum had thought? He doubted it.

Hours later, after a delicious steak, biscuits, and beans supper, followed up with dried fruit and coffee spiked with just a splash of whiskey—Pete figured Slocum wasn't trying to pull over anything on him by then—the men prepared their respective bedrolls along opposite sides of the fire. Slocum arranged his weapons close at hand and the old man said, "You always arm yourself to the teeth, fella? I ain't fixing to rob you in your sleep."

"I know that, but I do like to be prepared for anything that might try to surprise me."

"I hear that, Slocum. But I'm too blamed old to concern myself with such things anymore. If someone's going to rob me, what in the hell do they think they're going to get out of it? I got a mule who's ornerier than two wives, a suit of buckskins that never needs washing, and a poke that doesn't even exist anymore."

Slocum tilted his hat over his eyes, relieved that he was about to fall asleep at last. It had been a long few days on the trail.

"Course, that don't apply where the Devil Woman of the Rockies is concerned."

Slocum tilted his hat back on his head, propped himself up on an elbow. "You can't just say something like and not follow up with an explanation, Pete. What did you mean by 'Devil Woman of the Rockies'? You'll pardon me, but I've never heard of her."

Whiskey Pete said nothing, just arranged a rope around the perimeter of his bedroll, making sure it was a smooth, even distance all around.

"I thought that was for rattlesnakes," said Slocum.

"Who says it ain't?"

Slocum smiled and lay back down. He let a minute of silence go by, then said, "So who's this 'Devil Woman' anyway?"

"By God, but you don't give up on a thing, do you?" Pete sighed a long, drawn-out sound as if what he was about to reveal might cost him a lot of money. "Okay, then, but don't come whining to me when you can't sleep for the next two weeks!"

"So?"

Another sigh, then: "She's a witchy thing, got hair clear

down to her feet, horn nubs have been spotted sticking up from it, and her skin's like a snake's—all scales and scars." Pete sat up, leaned on an elbow, and didn't seem to notice that he was warming to his topic. Slocum tried to keep a straight face.

"They say she don't like people snoopin' around her mountains, that she'll kill a man and drain his blood like you or me might . . ."

"Drain a cup of coffee?"

"Okay, mister. You go ahead and mock me, but I'm telling you—this ain't no laughing matter. She never leaves people alive."

"Then how do you know so much about her?"

"Well . . . people I know have seen her."

"So *they* lived through an encounter with her, eh?"

The old man wagged a finger at Slocum in the firelight. "I know what you're driving at, you wiseacre. And I'm here to tell you that she's as real as you or me. The Cree don't much like her. Call her taboo, say she's tainted and crazy and evil and all manner of things ain't fit for civilized ears to hear. Now you just keep a sharp eye when you go up into them mountains."

"I will, Whiskey Pete. You bet I will. Say, the Rockies is a pretty big range for one Devil Woman, isn't it?"

"Aw." The old man tossed a stick at Slocum. "Get to sleep. I ain't telling you no more cautionary tales. Figured it was my duty. Didn't want to know I'd sent you on your way without fair warning. I couldn't bear to be with myself, now could I?"

Slocum realized he'd been gently poking fun at the old man when Pete was genuinely concerned for his safety in the face of this "Devil Woman."

"I appreciate it, Pete. I really do. And I promise you I'll keep a sharp eye out for her."

"Well, see that you do." And within a minute, the old man was sawing logs like the practice would soon go out of fashion.

Slocum lay awake for some time, wondering not much about

the Devil Woman of the Rockies, but quite a bit about the conundrum Delbert Calkins was rapidly becoming. Was he or wasn't he an experienced trailsman? Where was he headed? Did he have any gear? Slocum's mind chewed on these thoughts as he drifted off to sleep, despite the old man's rattling snores.

9

After a hearty breakfast in which Slocum had offered up more of his supplies for the two of them to enjoy, the old man kicked back for what looked to Slocum like a nap.

He busied himself with cleaning up the rest of his gear, packing it onto the horses, and when he was about ready to hit the trail, he tossed a sack of Arbuckle's on the man's belly. The old coot erupted in a yowl and had his knife and tomahawk half shucked from his belt when he saw Slocum grinning down at him.

"What's this all about, then?"

"Coffee for you. I figured that with your hospitality and those fine steaks, it was the least I could do."

"I can't take such a fine gift," said Pete, but his bony hands were caressing the sack as if he'd been given a poke brimming with gold.

"Yes, you can. And now I have to light on out."

"You make it back this way, you look me up. I'm right fond of this spot. Might stay for a while. Got me a wind break, Ethel's got a bit of browse, and the game trail yonder keeps me in fresh meat. What more could a man want?"

"Coffee!" said Slocum, mounting up.

"Exactly. And if you wait long enough, even that comes to you." Whiskey Pete grinned and ambled over to Slocum, the sack of coffee tucked under one bony wing. He reached up and shook Slocum's hand. "You take care now, and mind what I said."

"I will. And if I catch up with that fella I'm after, I'll make gentle inquiries about your poke."

"Just the stone, Slocum. He's welcome to the rest. I would like my pretty blue stone back."

"I'll do my best, Pete." He touched his hat brim and headed on out toward the mountains. After a few yards, he said, "I'll give the Devil Woman your regards!"

"Confound it, you numbskull! It ain't no laughin' matter!" But even Pete had to chuckle as Slocum rode off.

A few miles up the trail, Slocum reached into his coat pocket for his makings and felt a bulge in his breast pocket that wasn't familiar. He quickly reached in and tweezered out the odd item with his fingers. It was a small carved wolf. The detail was remarkable. He admired the palm-sized carving for a few minutes, then carefully stowed it back in his pocket. "Whiskey Pete," he said, rolling a quirley and squinting at the far-off peaks.

It felt good to be in higher country, and within sight of ever-bigger mountains again. His work during much of the preceding six months had taken him through some pretty flat country, and while it had is own charms, he missed the mountains. The sight of them made him feel confident somehow that he would succeed on this almost wild-goose chase. The only thing he found annoying about mountains was that once they were in sight, it seemed to take years to reach them.

He rode, head bent to his right in an effort to deflect the steady south-headed wind from his face. He rode for another four hours and it felt as if they were still the same distance away, though he knew better. Then there would be a point when he'd look up and they'd suddenly appear, as if conjured closer than ever.

And that point was almost on him. Try as he might, there

were no decent tracks on the plains and into the foothills. Nothing to let him know that a man on horseback had passed this way some days before. But he had—that much Slocum knew. He hadn't seen any sign of tracks cutting north or south. However, the wind here could be tremendous at times and they had had fresh snows, at least three in the past week. Pete was clear about that.

Slocum hoped he'd have better luck at locating tracks once he got deeper into the foothills. It had been a long time since he'd been this far north, but it struck him again, as it always did when he fell to musing about man-made divisions, just how borders like that between the United States and Canada became decided.

He knew all about war and staking claims and surveying, but who really decided such things? And once people settled in an area, what made them take on such a pride of place? People proudly claimed they were from some place, a state or territory, when really it was all just one big ol' landscape.

He shook his head and smiled at his folly. "The things I get to thinking about when I'm on the trail," he said aloud to his horse. As they climbed between two sizable swells that led into high timber country, he glanced down to make sure they weren't heading into a rocky draw. And that's when he saw the tracks.

They were not that old, still well preserved, and only partly filled in with blown snow. And they were two of a horse's hooves and, between them, the tracks of a man's boot. He dismounted and tied the horses off to a scrub pine. As he squatted to inspect the prints, his heart pounded harder. Could it be that he'd found Delbert's tracks after weeks on the trail? There weren't all that many people foolish enough to be out in these parts in midwinter. He squatted down and peeled off a glove.

As he poked at the boot prints, he knew for certain they weren't Whiskey Pete's tracks. The old man had worn fur-wrapped moccasins, in keeping with his buckskin attire, and these tracks were made by a boot, flat heel, not too tall, decent for riding, and not the boots of a town dandy. He stood and placed his own boot gently over the one fully visible track. He'd been told that he and Delbert Calkins were roughly the same height and build, and this print supported that notion.

Slocum bent low again and followed the tracks forward. The only reason they were visible at all was that he was now out of the incessant wind. Even the horses seemed to appreciate it and stood hip-shot, as if enjoying the warm winter sun without the ceaseless wind accompanying it.

As he made his way on foot farther up the declivity, he was rewarded with more tracks where the wind hadn't sluiced in and blown snow across them. "One set's better than any others," he said to himself. "Especially when that's all you have, Slocum."

He made his way back to the horses and led them on foot up the small pass. The tracks, man and horse, were enough in evidence that he could guess where they were headed by looking ahead. Scanning the area, he chose the route he would have taken, and lo and behold, that's where the tracks went. Pretty soon, though, the man's tracks ceased and the horse's tracks dented deeper into the crust. That meant Delbert had mounted up and Slocum decided to do the same. He still had about two hours of daylight left. He'd keep on going, find a decent spot to camp, and hope that any new snowfall didn't cover what was turning out to be a fine gift of tracks.

He trekked for longer than he'd anticipated, and by the time he made camp, he had accomplished three things: He'd lost sight of the track trail, though he had a pretty good idea it ran right by where he'd hunker for the night. He'd ended up with nearly no daylight in which to unsaddle the horses. And he'd also made it deep into the mountains, climbing steadier and growing colder. He could tell by the way they rose and fell far before him that the peaks he was now nestled among, big as they seemed, were but the foothills to the bigger looming peaks ahead.

He also knew that there would soon be lowlands and valleys he would cross. Maybe he'd come across Pete's band of Cree. They sounded to Slocum like a breakaway group. He'd heard of such high-mountain tribes, though only in passing. Some men said such isolated bands could be willing to tolerate strangers in their midst, jovial even, if the stranger had something worth trading for. Others said such tribes could be sullen, given to stripping a traveler bare of his goods, then setting him free to forage and die.

He would do well, Slocum decided, to play it close to the vest and maintain a quiet presence while on their land. The last thing he needed was to mix it up with Indians. Any party of two outnumbered him by double. You toss in an entire tribe's worth of braves and there's no telling how poorly he'd fare in a square-off.

By his reckoning, Slocum had been in Canada for more than a week, heading northwest the entire time. He had no doubt that his quarry knew someone was tracking him; otherwise the man would not have continued at such a foolhardy pace, and in such a foolhardy direction. Then again, reasoned Slocum, I am no less a fool for sticking with him all this way. So far he'd not been able to get within sight of the man, but that disappointment worked in his favor, too, as that meant Calkins hadn't been able to see him, nor peel off a shot in his direction.

It rankled Slocum that he had lost the man's trail in the high country. That squall just as dark descended the night before had wiped out any sign he might have picked up. Despite that, he felt a renewed sense of hope. Tomorrow was a new day and he still felt strong. He'd suspected for some days that Delbert's unexpected impressive strength of will had begun to flag.

How he knew this, Slocum couldn't say just yet, but it was there, an unspoken sign, something nibbling at the edges of the chase. Maybe the odd sound that might trail back to him on a stiff breeze, or with the tracks that day, perhaps it had been the slight lengthening of the man's strides in the snow.

Slocum crouched in the snow in a nearly cold camp, warming stiff hands over a fire big enough for melting snow to make coffee. He chose the spot at the base of a low jagged rock overhang so that he would not be ambushed from behind. As for the front, he'd sleep with one eye open. He told himself he was waiting for Calkins to rouse himself and begin his day.

Wanting bacon, but not wanting to send any such aroma up on a breeze, even though the breeze was with him, Slocum denied the growling in his gut and waited for the coffee to bubble. He rubbed one hand over the other, gathering what heat he could as if scooping it from the very air. He rolled another quirley and his thoughts of food led him to once again to recall the odd series of events that led him to this foolhardy job.

A smile spread over his face. "The things I do for women," he said to his little campfire.

He crouched over his small fire, sipped his coffee, and nibbled on a couple of hard biscuits and jerky, some dried fruit. But what he really wanted was more of a sign of that damned Delbert Calkins. The tracks from earlier had only served to whet his appetite. He itched for sight of the man, a confrontation.

This elusiveness annoyed him, and given that he was still untold days behind the man, not seeming to gain on him was vexing. Slocum knew he wasn't the world's best tracker, though he was a fair hand at it when pressed, but the tracks of today didn't seem to him to be much older than three or four days. Maybe he had gained a day on the man.

With that hopeful thought on his mind, Slocum drifted off to a short, fitful night's sleep. He had no way of knowing that it would be the last decent night's sleep he'd get in a long time.

The next day found him up and on the trail early, just as the rising sun glinted warmth onto the shadowed silver of the crusted slopes all around him. He began the day by leading the Appaloosa and packhorse, as much to get his own blood pumping as to give the Appaloosa a chance to stretch his own legs before Slocum climbed into the saddle.

Up, then down, up, down—he'd no sooner crest another

rise than he'd descend again in a switchback pattern. The steeper the hillsides grew, the more switchbacks he was forced to cut. Far below, on the last rise before the larger mountains rose up in jaw-dropping height before him, there lay a small vale.

Along its bottom, a river coursed through as though black yarn had been drizzled along the floor of the valley. It looked to him to be a perfect spot to camp, and maybe Delbert thought the same thing—maybe there would be sign down along the half-frozen river. Especially given that the man probably didn't know he was being followed. He might suspect something, but Slocum doubted Calkins knew for certain that he was on his trail.

Though he'd seen a few border rivers that flowed south to north, given the rising height of the surrounding landscape, this one flowed in the expected north to south fashion, grinding along—even from this height thousands of feet above, he fancied he could hear it roiling and gnashing its way down through the high mountains.

And that's when the massive black shape emerged as if by magic from the snowed slope just a dozen yards below where they stood. A grizzly nosing out of its den—but in winter? What was the brute doing coming out of hibernation now? Had he disturbed it?

But Slocum had no more time for speculation, because the Appaloosa caught sight of the bear, then seemed to transmit its instant fear, expressed in screaming, lunging up on its hind legs. It sent its fear through the lead line right to the packhorse.

Thus far the packhorse had proven to be a perfect trail horse, almost seeming to anticipate Slocum's own moves and judgments, and did it all without complaint. Even the Appaloosa seemed downright scatterbrained in the packhorse's presence.

But all that changed when the big, angry grizz emerged from his den, chuffing and with ears flattened. It seemed he'd gone to bed in a bad mood and woken up—for whatever reason—in an even worse mood.

The Appy lunged and twice nearly unseated Slocum before a third lunge combined with its back feet sliding downslope. Slocum knew what was about to happen, saw the shrubs and talus slope below rise up to meet him. He had a quick flash of memory of the burly Indian woman he'd shot, of her boot stuck in the stirrup, and he kicked free just as he landed hard on his right shoulder.

He knew that the Appaloosa and so, the packhorse, might soon follow him downslope if they kept on in the same bewildered fashion they'd been acting, so he kept on rolling with it, and at the same time tried to claw a Colt free of its holster.

The grizzly kept on emerging from its den and to Slocum it seemed the biggest he'd ever seen. When it finally swung its head around and caught sight of the mayhem happening just above it on the slope, the first thing it did was open its mouth wide and bellow.

Those teeth looked like long, curved things a doctor might use to pry open a gut-shot man. It tore after him in a flash and almost immediately experienced the same thing his horse had—the grizzly's back feet slid right out from under it. Slocum took the opportunity to gain his feet and back up as fast as he could, shucking both Colts and slipping free the leather thong he kept tied about the hilt of his Bowie knife when traveling.

The bear seemed not to care about the two horses that were already well past the two of them and headed at a long slant downslope. Slocum wondered, if he lived through the encounter, if he would be able to track them down along the river below.

But right now he had more pressing concerns—like how to outwit a grizzly dead-set on ripping his head off.

"Whoa, bear! Whoa, bear!" he shouted, backing up and shaking his pistols before him in an effort to appear even half as menacing as the bear. It wasn't working.

Thankfully the bear was either still half-dazed from his hibernatory sleep or just having a plain old hard time keeping his footing on the slick sheen of crusted snow. But it was gaining on him. Slocum looked around—there was nowhere to go but down, and at the rate he needed to make it, the run would be a treacherous and foolhardy thing to do—and just what he decided he had to do. But only until he made it to that boulder knobbed halfway out of the slope a hundred yards down to the left. Could he make it there before the grizzly made it to him?

Already the beast was closing the gap between them. Slocum saw its thick cinnamon-tinged coat ripple and swing. The bear had lost some weight sleeping but was still in fine shape, must have gone into its den fat and happy. Its nose twitched and worked left to right, up and down, like an animal with a mind of its own, the nostrils quivering and taking in every scent imaginable.

Slocum knew his next move, even as he bolted downslope. He would shoot the thing. He hated to, not because it would bother him to kill the bear, but because he'd probably only end up pissing it off in good shape—the one thing you didn't want when an angry grizzly was on your tail was a *wounded* angry grizzly. Things would go from bad to horrible in the time it took to squeeze a trigger.

Maybe he would get the chance to empty his guns into the beast. He had made it halfway to the boulder, where he hoped he might be able to play cat-and-mouse with it, at least to keep it between them long enough for him to squeeze off shots straight into its mouth and eyes. He had no better plan than that. And if the thing landed on him, pawing and slashing, he always had the knife. The damn bear might well end up killing him, but he'd do his best to make it follow him shortly.

He was less than twenty feet from the rock when he glanced over his shoulder and knew he wasn't going to make it. The grizz was one stride away from him, its massive shoulder hunch wagging, front muscles bunching and rippling, and its claws lashing outward with each forward dive. It was covering twice the ground he was with every stride.

Slocum kept on downslope and reached under his left arm with his right and squeezed off two shots. One lead pill must have found its furry mark because he heard a deeper throaty roar just behind his head. Then something pushed into him low in his back and sent him whipping forward right past that boulder, his last chance at slim survival.

As his body slammed face-first downslope, he felt something inside give way. And then his head hit and a dazed sensation immediately flooded his senses, as if bells were gonging through his body though he couldn't hear much else. Still he whipped forward, kept on rolling down the steep slide. He had a vague idea that if he could keep on rolling, he might be able to make it all the way down to the river, then float on out of there, away from the grizzly . . .

But something was wrong. His head cleared, and the single worst stink he'd ever smelled clouded his senses. He cracked open an eye and at the same time his hearing partially came back. Blasting stink and raw, angry sounds at him, the grizzly was an inch from his face, its massive black-pink lips hanging like cutaway flesh, those teeth curving upward, every other one either broken off or jagged at the tip. They were brown at the base, turning to yellow in the middle, then a gleaming bone color wet with spittle, and the liver-colored tongue between thrashed like a flat serpent.

Then lightning struck Slocum's right leg and hot, blazing pain flowered up his side from just above his knee. At the same time, even more sound rushed in with the speed of an oncoming steam engine, and he came out of his daze fully, wishing to God he were somewhere else.

Somehow in his tumble he had lost his Colts. The bear swung its head over him as if trying to hypnotize him with its ferocity. The massive beast's hair-covered hide clouded out everything else—even air. Its reek was stifling, but Slocum's least concern was how bad the air smelled. This thing was about to open him up like a kill-crazy drunkard with a skinning knife in one hand and an empty bottle in the other.

Why hadn't it lunged at him yet? It seemed more intent on threatening him, warning him, as if it were just angry but not willing to kill. Nah, he knew that was his mind lying to him. This beast was just working itself up to kill.

Slocum's hand scrabbled low—not like the bear was going to see what he was doing, straddling him as it was—and he prayed his Bowie knife was still with him—and it was. He felt the familiar handle with his benumbed hand; already the knife had worked itself halfway out of the sheath. Just in time. Slocum wrapped his fingers around it just as the bear leaned back as if to drive itself down at him. On the opposite side of his body as Slocum's knife, the bear raised a head-size paw. Curved, daggerlike claws each as long as a man's fingers were spread wide and arcing down at his face—now or never!

Slocum held fast to the knife and swung his arm over and across himself, in his own wide arc, trying to beat the bear's foreleg to the strike. He succeeded in ramming the blade, its keen edge slicing deep into the bear's foreleg. The knife lodged in bone, but the bear's quick reaction, coupled with a roar of agonized rage, nearly jerked the knife from Slocum's grasp.

He held firm and the bear slumped backward for the span of a few heartbeats, howling and roaring its rage, not comprehending what this thing was that dared bite back. And then it came onto him again and this time wasted no time in posturing above him, but lunged with its terrible mouth straight at him, sinking fangs into his left shoulder and pulling back with its mouth part-closed. It lifted Slocum with its head up off the blood-soaked snow.

Hot agony such as he'd never felt flooded Slocum's mind and body, and he nearly lost consciousness. Even with its mouth clamped over his shoulder, the beast's bellowing roar was deafening. Slocum's face was mashed into the bear's neck. He tried to grit his teeth, tasting the hair, feeling it crowding into his mouth and nose. The grizzly shook him, rattling every bone in his body, ripping into the meat of his shoulder more with each swing of its mighty head.

Slocum felt wetness and numbness seep into his body from the wound, knew he would pass out soon if he didn't make a stand. The knife, he remembered the knife, and with what he was sure was the last of his waning strength, mustered from the very soles of his boots, he screamed bloody murder into the bear's ear and drove the knife into the bear's dense hide over and over.

The first few strikes didn't seem to faze the brute, but Slocum kept on ramming the Bowie's blood-slick blade into the gore-soaked fur, over and over. Finally the bear opened its mouth and dropped Slocum to the ground, where he thudded onto his back, dazed, weak, but with his dripping steel held aloft. The bear, bloody mouth wide open, roared and lunged at him again, backed off when it felt the blade hack at its snout, then seemed to give up caring altogether and drove its face once again at him.

Just when it seemed as if it was about to close its bawling maw on Slocum's face, the brute whipped its massive head skyward and roared louder than ever. Then Slocum heard it— gunshots from far off—and felt the impact of the bullets slamming into the grizzly's hide. He didn't dare move, didn't dare distract it from the obvious pain the bullets were causing.

Over and over he heard the far-off shots, evenly spaced and well aimed, from the sight of the beast's quivering reactions and howls of rage and pain. Soon, the bear's steady roars dwindled to clipped growls, then became grunts, and all the while it swayed, looked drunk, confused, and angry all at once.

Slocum's vision was blurring and he felt his strength waning. Would he expire along with the bear? Had he lost that much blood? Surely the bear had. And who had done the shooting? Sounded like a Sharps buffalo gun . . .

He noticed the creature had ceased its rumbling moan, and he forced his eyes open to see what that might mean. Slocum saw the great bear still poised over him, but leaning as if about to topple—on him.

A desperate surge of strength jolted Slocum awake, and he knew he had to slide himself out from under the damn bear—or he would find himself trapped under a thousand pounds of dead, stinking, bleeding grizzly.

But try as he might, he couldn't push himself away from the bear. As he watched, it all happened as if the hands of a clock were magically slowed. A last shot, echoing up the steep slope, drove like a hidden fist into the bear's neck. He saw it enter, watched meat and hair and blood and bone burst out the other side of the bear's body. With a last agonizing roar, the bear wobbled and crashed straight down on top of him, trapping the knife he'd raised at the last second, and driving the hilt into its gut.

All the air left Slocum's body in a fast wheeze the second the bear dropped on him. It took but another couple of seconds for the bear to finally succumb to his many wounds from bullet and knife. It sagged all over him, it seemed, and Slocum knew for certain he was about to expire himself. Then he felt something pop near his gut, felt a sudden warm rush all over him. What was that?

The knife, of course, he told himself. He'd been stupid to hold that knife upright at the last second, as if it might help him somehow. But the bear's near-dead weight had driven it into him, dull end first. And yet, it had punctured the beast's belly just below the rib cage and now its life juices, its guts, were forcing their way out. He still couldn't breathe, but it gave him an idea, and he wasted no time in pursuing it.

With what little leverage he had, Slocum worked his aching hand, the hilt of the knife grinding into his own gut. He wasn't sure what he was trying to accomplish, but that hand was the only thing still able to move, despite the bear's weight atop him. A trickle of air still wheezed in and out of Slocum's mouth, but it was a fight he was quickly losing as the bear's weight crushed his chest.

The knife blade, always honed to a paper-slicing edge, made grim progress into the dead brute's gut cavity. Keep cutting, keep cutting, he told himself. Maybe you'll have enough luck to slice your arm free, grab the snowy upslope, and gain leverage enough to push the dead bear off you . . .

But he knew it was an effort doomed to failure. Already he was slipping away again into unconsciousness. And this time, he knew he would not rouse from it.

10

When Delbert Calkins stumbled upon the Cree's encampment, they seemed surprised to see him, though he knew they had watched him for some time. No doubt they were suspicious—rightfully so, as he was a stranger in their midst.

That very day on the trail, his horse had just about given up the ghost, as his old grandfather used to say. He knew he'd abused it for far longer than he should have, so when he saw the little village—the smoking fire pit in the middle of it all, the few trees here and there with bits of hide and decoration hanging from them, the dark-haired people wrapped in colorful blankets and furs gathering outside in the snow to stare at him—he knew they were his only hope for survival.

Delbert kept on jamming his heels into that stupid horse's gut until it just stopped lifting its feet up out of the chest-high holes it had been punching in the granular snow.

He sat on the thing, pounding it with his hands, his boots, drumming hard against the belly of the beast. But other than groans and long, snot-filled wheezes, he got nothing more from the horse. Soon it just plain collapsed beneath him, but it didn't slump down far, as the snow held it up. And then it died. Right there at the top of the hill, overlooking the valley with the river and the Indian camp, so close to salvation and the dumb horse dies.

He kept looking at the Indians, but they only stared at him across the bare little valley, across the river, and up to where he'd crested the ridge overlooking their camp. Didn't even make motions of coming to his rescue. What good were they?

And so he had to climb down off the dead horse, unstrap his saddlebags, and after double-checking that the familiar bulge in his coat was still there (as he did at least one hundred times a day to remind himself he still had the money from that little Garfield snip's foolish father), high-stepped down the steep slope toward the river below.

He only made it halfway down when he lost his footing and tumbled, as his old grandfather had also said, "ass over bandbox" to the bottom. On coming to a painful rest up against a boulder, his first thought had been about the money. Another pat, though he made sure to do it without the Indians seeing, and he was pleased to note it was okay.

He spluttered up out of the snow only to see the Indians still staring at him, and though it was too far for him to see well, he didn't think they were laughing at him.

He also made sure his side arm made it through okay. The holster was closed at the end and the handle strapped down securely. The derringer in an inner coat pocket was still there, too. He might not know much about how to keep that damn horse from killing itself, but he damn sure knew how to use a gun.

And he was sure that despite the fact that he'd gotten turned around, he would soon be on his way. Precisely because he had guns and money. The only things he needed now were food, warmth, and some way out of the damned mountains, a direction toward the Mississippi River, where he could gamble away his "earnings" and figure out where to go, what to do next.

Delbert was also sure that he'd been tailed and chased into the mountains by someone. It was as much a feeling as anything of proof and with substance, but it was such feelings that had kept him alive on the streets of Chicago all those years.

He finally made it across the half-frozen river and the barren flat beyond, and up to the gathered Indians. He hoped to God this tribe was friendly. If not, he felt sure he could take out six, perhaps eight counting his two-shot derringer. But without adequate cover so he might reload, he stood no chance. The ones standing in the front looked to be male and most of them cradled rifles in their arms. He would be lucky indeed, he figured, if they left him alone and unharmed.

They finally shifted their features as he approached. A dog came yipping toward him. One of the men uttered a short, sharp bark of his own and the dog stopped, tail tucked, and retreated. Delbert had slung his saddlebags over his shoulder and now approached with caution, his hands raised and a smile on his face. He drew to within forty feet of the gathered Indians.

He saw their peculiar eyes, dark and liquid, their equally dark hair, silky black and pulled back. It looked as if some of them wore it greased. It was a warmish day for winter, so most of them did not wear any headgear, but he did see a couple of men who wore fur hats.

"Hello there, friends," he said, trying to look frightened and worried. He even glanced once or twice back over his shoulder. "I am Delbert Calkins. And I am in desperate need of help. A vicious killer is on my trail and I have nowhere else to turn."

11

Slocum heard a voice, a human voice, as if spoken through water, through gravel, through thunder. It was saying something . . . but what? Was this death? Was this all there was to the long, long game everyone fought so hard to be part of?

He could not see, could barely hear, and yet he . . . felt . . . warmth, and cold and touch? Was something touching him? He worked so very hard to open his eyes, to try to break free from this dream, but it was impossible. And then he slept.

It was a voice again that woke him. And this time he knew he was not dead. At least he thought he wasn't. He'd been wrong before about a good many things, so why not now? But something again touched him, dragged across his face, his arms . . . snakes? He worked to open his eyes, vaguely aware that he had tried to do this before and had failed.

Light, gray and fuzzy, wormed its way into his eyes. He pictured a small version of himself pushing his heavy eyelids apart, his muscles straining with the effort, and it worked. All at once they fluttered like a moth's wings, opened, and in the dim, yellow light haloed over his head, he saw a grinning face leaning down close.

He found his voice, heard what he'd intended as a scream come out instead as a whisper, and he said, "Devil Woman of the Rockies . . ."

The mouth of the wavering, leering face opened wide and he heard the same watery whooshing sounds that began to sound a whole lot like low, drawn-out laughter. That was the last thing Slocum remembered for a long time.

Something touched his lips, woke him. It was hot, burned him. He flinched, tried to recoil, but the movement only brought pain. He heard himself whisper, "What . . . what is it?"

"Broth." Then as an afterthought, the voice said, "For your throat." It was a soft voice, a woman's voice, but there was a hard edge to it, the voice of someone who would brook no foolishness.

"Who are you?" He made his eyes open, and everything blurred, came back into focus briefly, then fuzzed out again, as if he were looking at the bright sun though gauzy white curtains that kept blowing back and forth across an open window. The light hurt, but he wanted it to, wanted to take it all in. Surely he wasn't dead. This looked too real—the inside of a cabin? He tried to move, and felt the pain again. It seemed to come from all over him, through him, lancing and piercing and throbbing all at once.

"You are alive, in case you were wondering."

The voice came from his left side. He tried to turn his head, felt the pain again.

"Stop doing that."

"What?" he wheezed through gritted teeth.

"Moving. I didn't work for two days to get you patched up so you could rip apart your wounds."

"Who are you? Where am I?"

He heard the voice sigh. It was definitely a woman's voice. And not as hard as he'd imagined. But where was she? Then he heard footsteps, boots on wood, and the silhouette of someone blotting out the light from the far window, but the light outlined a form, slender with long hair.

Then she pulled the long hair back, gathering it in one hand, and reached up with the other, tied it back with something. Then she leaned down over him. "I am Sigrid Berglund."

It was a foreign name, Scandinavian, and her voice bore the strong trace of an accent from such a place.

"And you are John Slocum," she said.

He stared at her without speaking, trying to puzzle out who she was, what he was doing there, why he hurt so badly.

"You were expecting . . . the Devil Woman of the Rockies perhaps?"

"What? What does that mean?"

"You really don't remember, do you?"

"No. Tell me what's going on here."

"That was the first thing you called me. Devil Woman of the Rockies. I thought it was funny. You are almost dead and the first thing you choose to say to me is that. Insult your savior, good plan, Mr. Slocum." She laughed, a sound like ringing bells, but bold, with a confidence he'd rarely heard in a woman's voice.

"Savior? From what?"

"I will say one word and you will probably remember. Maybe not." She shrugged. "But we have to start somewhere, okay?"

He tried to nod, but it hurt. He whispered, "Okay."

She cleared her throat and said, "Bear."

He almost thought she was playing a joke on him, then something, like water dripping through an earthen dam, popped through. The drips became more drips, became a trickle, then a steady stream, then a spurt. Before he knew it, the mud gave way and memories of what had happened flooded his mind.

Slocum's eyes flew wide open, and he jammed himself back into the bedding hard, wincing at the pain, but needing it, needing its reassuring lancing comfort to remind him that he had fought that grizzly and lived. Somehow, impossibly, with that foul death-dealing beast dead on top of him, he had lived . . . but only because someone had helped.

Someone, he remembered now, with a Sharps rifle had blasted the bear methodically, unmercifully until it had expired on top of him.

"You . . . You shot the bear?"

She stood upright again, folded her arms in front of her. "Is that so difficult to believe, Mr. Slocum?"

He almost chuckled. "Nothing is difficult to believe anymore."

"Good," she said.

And though he still hadn't seen her face because the light was at her back and he was in a darkened corner, he could tell she was smiling.

"Now, let's get some of this broth into you before you shrivel into nothing. And then the bear will have won. This we cannot let happen, right?"

This time he did nod. "Right." Then other things occurred to him, things he needed answers to. "My horses . . ."

"They are fine, a few bruises and sore limbs from sliding and running down the slope, but I have tended to them. They are sheltered in my barn."

"And my things, everything the horses carried? My guns?"

"Also fine. I took the liberty of unpacking your gear and have stored what was not necessary. I used what I needed— your clothes, that sort of thing. The guns and the rest of your possessions I have over there." She nodded to a spot across the room. "You may have them when you are well. Now enough talk. You must eat."

12

Within a couple of days, Slocum was well enough to sit up, feed himself with his right arm, and take whatever nourishment Sigrid brought to him. She tended to all his basic needs, changed the bandages on his wounds, and from what he saw, she did a masterful job at stitching up the puncture marks on his shoulder, chest, and arm. The grizzly had also raked his right thigh and landed a few lesser gouges along his abdomen. But even these she tended to, not with a foul-smelling goop he'd seen so many people use, but with pleasant-smelling tinctures and liniments.

"Where did you learn your doctoring skills?"

She did not respond, merely smiled.

Yes, sir. She was dutiful in just about everything, but she was not talkative. Getting her to engage in conversation was like talking to a tree stump. A pretty one, to be sure, but a quiet one.

Still, she did not seem perturbed with him. On the contrary, she hummed while she worked, sang softly to herself, even in front of him. She smiled at him as she changed his dressings, without a self-conscious bone in her body. Almost as if she'd not grown up in the company of others. She was a puzzle to him, and one he figured he'd try to decipher, if only because he had been injured badly in the past, and he knew healing took time.

When she did speak, it was with an air of education, as if she'd been to a fine college back East. But if she hadn't, the evidence of a homegrown education nestled here in the mountains was all around—the walls were covered with shelves of books.

"How did you get so many books up here in the mountains?"

She smiled at him, kept on humming. By now he knew not to expect an answer. Or if he did get one, it would come later, unexpectedly, and would be brief. Almost as if she considered everything he said. It made him begin to consider his questions to her.

True to form, she spoke some minutes after he had asked his question—so much later that he initially didn't know just what she was talking about.

"My father. He was a professor back East. They are his books."

Slocum nodded. So that meant either her father was dead, missing, or had just retired from being a professor and was about the place somewhere. Or any other explanation he'd not thought of. Either way, it didn't really matter. He wasn't one to pry into other people's lives. He was curious about her, however. And that combination made him all the more eager to learn about her.

But he contented himself with watching her as she worked. He still slept a great deal, figured it was his body's way of healing, but he was thankful that her tinctures and salves did an incredible job of keeping the pain at bay. Without her help, he would be dead. Even if he'd managed to survive the bear attack, he would most likely have died of fever beside a paltry little fire at the bottom of the slope. No sir, he owed this woman a great deal. She had saved his life and was still doing it.

Sigrid was a tall, well-built woman, muscled, Slocum assumed, from years of tending to everything for herself—evidence of her father being alive had not shown itself. The wonder of it all was that she was continually smiling, humming, and singing. Hauling wood, carrying water, cutting meat, tending the stove, and changing his dressings.

It was on the third day after he awoke that he thought he heard dogs growling and maybe even a yip or bark. He asked her about it.

"They are my sled dogs." Then she went back to baking bread.

Now he was more curious than ever. Who was this woman? Unfortunately he spent another few days in near silence, drifting in and out of restive sleep, feeling better with each passing day. He spent some of the time trying to read a book she had brought him, pleased that he had requested such a thing. "I am capable of reading, you know," he said, offering a smile.

"Of course you can. No man worth anything in life could be illiterate."

Was that a compliment? An insult? He had no idea, but try as he might, he couldn't concentrate on the words, not so much because of the pain, but because he couldn't keep from thinking about Delbert Calkins and how foolish the entire chase had suddenly become in his mind. He'd gone off more for his own reasons than for any particular quest for justice. And it had nearly gotten him killed, given him injuries such that every time he took off his shirt, he'd be reminded.

That afternoon she came to his bedside and said, "You will begin walking today, Mr. Slocum. And tomorrow you will sauna."

"What was that I will do?" He assumed from her laugh that alarm was evident on his face, but he didn't care.

"I will build up the fire and we will purify and cleanse our bodies with a sauna."

His look still expressed confusion, he was sure, so she continued, "It is a small building out by the pond. I will build up the fire and we will sit in the steam. It is good for our bodies, our minds. You see?"

"Sure," he said. In fact, he was familiar with such

proceedings, but she was so pretty when she laughed, and he wanted to keep her talking.

Later, she got him up on his feet, and with his right arm draped over her shoulders, he took a few steps. The leg the grizzly had raked was tender, but in no danger of opening up. His shoulder, however, was still mighty sore. Most of all, he felt a little weak from not having been up and around in so long. "How long," he said, grimacing and shuffling forward away from the bed with her help, "have I been here anyway?"

"More than a week," she said.

That stopped him cold in his tracks. "What?"

"Yes, you do not remember it, because there were several days when you were unconscious. At first you were full of the coldness that can seep deep into the bones of someone close to death. And then you were filled with the fever and I feared you might die."

"I know I haven't said it properly, and I don't know as I can ever say it fully, nor repay your kindness, Sigrid, but—"

She shook her head. "No, no, I will not hear thanks for gratitude. It is just the way it had to be. No more, no less."

He wasn't sure what to make of such a statement, but he let it go for now. He owed her his life, and that wasn't something he'd let go unacknowledged.

They were in the kitchen now of the house, and it was sunnier, brighter, and more cheerful than he had expected. It was not at all like so many other settlers' cabins, all chinked logs and few windows and filled with smoke. This place was very well constructed. He admired every detail now that he was able to see more than the closed-off sleeping space.

The logs had all been squared off and fitted neatly together with the hands of a craftsman. The chinking was light colored, nearly white—he guessed there was lime in the mix. And the roof, from what he saw between the rafters, was a sod affair, but it was not messy and hanging down in sloppy strands. This one was tucked up there neat and tidy as you please.

The biggest surprise he saw as he inched his way around the long, polished wooden table and chairs were the windows. They were many and multipaned, like you might see in houses in a town. But way up here? It must have taken a month of Sundays to get them here—and a whole lot of money to buy them in the first place.

The rest of it was sparsely but comfortably furnished, with the sleeping area behind him built into a curtained alcove. He spied another alongside the handsome fireplace dominating the far end of the house.

"This place is beautiful, Sigrid. Did you build it?"

"No, not alone. My father was the builder. I merely helped him. As much as a child can."

"Your father sounds like quite an accomplished man."

"Yes," she said, running her hand along the table top absentmindedly. "Yes, he was very talented. Not only was he a scholar but a builder, an inventor." She looked at him, her smile resumed. "He was a great thinker."

"Not a bad tribute for a man to have," he said.

Slocum assumed the man was dead, but he didn't think she wanted to be asked about that just yet. Still, he was curious as to how they'd ended up here. He pushed down the curiosity and continued to take in the room's artistic features—red, blue, green, and white flowers were painted tastefully along the faces of some of the beams and wall logs, while others were carved richly into the beams themselves. The floor, too, was a planked affair, the wood worn smooth through years of use and labor and, as with everything else, kept spotlessly clean. The wood glowed a honeyed orange, as if he were walking on a light sunset.

"It is good that you are stronger than I suspected, because I would like to sauna. I believe, from the smell of you, that it would do you good as well. We shall sauna together."

"And when will this happen?" he said, still admiring the artfully built fireplace.

"Now."

He turned, forgetting his suspect balance. "Now?"

Sigrid resumed her place beside him, draped his arm over her shoulder. "Now."

She guided him to the door, a Dutch door, split horizontally in the middle and able to be opened from the top or bottom. But it being winter, the halves were joined as one door with a pretty curtained window in it allowing in diffuse light.

She led him outside, where he was pleased to see the day was sunny and warm, and the snow on the eaves was dripping. Sure, there was a whole lot of snow on the ground, but the fresh air felt so good on his face, he filled his lungs, coughed, tried again.

"You will have your strength back in no time, John Slocum."

"Good thing, too. You've been taking care of me long enough. I hate to be such a burden on anyone."

"It is no bother. I am here anyway. Most of the time alone, so . . . come, let me show you the barn. You can see your horses and meet my dogs."

The barn looked much the same as the house, now that he was outside and could give them both a going-over. Each had lime plaster between the logs, red painted shutters on the windows, and boxes hanging underneath, where he assumed in the warmer months flowers might be planted. Even the shoveled paths were tidy.

"Don't you have trouble with Indians?"

She looked at him as if he had guessed a secret of some sort. Then she smiled and shook her head. "No, the closest tribe, they are Cree, lives a few valleys away. But I was here first, in a manner of speaking. They used to winter elsewhere, but now they stay there year-round." She shrugged, still smiling, and tugged open the big barn door.

The Appaloosa perked up his ears and came to the front of his stall. He seemed genuinely pleased to see Slocum and gave him a good shove with his head that nearly knocked Slocum down. Sigrid held him up and scolded the horse in her native tongue, words Slocum didn't know the meaning of, but could well guess. He guessed the horse did, too, because the Appy hung his head and looked at the ground as if he'd been caught thieving hay.

Even the packhorse seemed pleased to see him. He noted again what a fine little animal it was, stout and built for the mountains. He recalled it had spooked far less than the Appaloosa when the bear had emerged from its den.

"Even though you don't want to hear it, I thank you for taking such good care of my horses," he said, rubbing the Appy's chin.

She smiled. "Come. We'll meet the dogs and then it's time for a sauna." She led him straight though the little barn to the other end, opened a smaller door set into the larger one, and immediately heard an excited low yowling.

There stood six long-haired snow dogs, looking almost like wolves but decidedly thicker and more doglike, from their ears and wider, shorter bodies to their varied-color coats. And they all looked very excited to see Sigrid. They were not chained but penned together in a low-walled enclosure that Slocum felt sure each could easily jump out of. Yet it looked so comfortable and inviting within it that he could see why they wouldn't bother.

"These are my babies," she said, with a wave of her hand to indicate the dogs. Each wagged a tail and panted in that peculiar way dogs have of making it seem as if they are smiling. "I will not trouble you with their names now, but maybe when you are feeling better, I can take you on a sled run. It is . . . exhilarating." Her face lit at the prospect of it.

"I'd like that very much." It was good to hear her talk—she'd said more in the last half hour than she had all week. Slocum stood for a moment, let the sun beat on his face. Considering his wounds, he felt damn good.

As if she could read his mind, she said, "Soon, you will feel even better. A sauna can cure things that no amount of medicines and herbs can. Come." This time she did not take his arm but preceded him on yet another cleared path behind the small barn that led to a path into the woods. They wound down a gentle slope through the trees, and not far from the barn, he began to hear a familiar sound—running water.

"The river?" he said, stepping with care. He did not want to lose his footing and end up slowing his healing process.

"Yes," she said. "Just ahead, though it is quiet now, much covered in ice."

Soon they emerged into a small clearing, sunny and with a sizable frozen pond in the middle. There was a small dock leading into the middle of it. On land, at the foot of the dock, sat a squat log building with a sod roof and aromatic smoke puffing out the chimney.

"Sauna?" he said.

She looked back at him and smiled.

13

Sigrid waited for him at the door of the little hut. Beside the door were two hooks with what looked like soft, large pieces of flannel hanging from them. She left him puzzling at the frozen-over pond, and Slocum began to get an inkling of what she had in mind for him. He wasn't entirely sure he wanted to know the full extent of her plans. He was about ready to head back up the trail to the house when she popped open the door and a cloud of cedar-smelling steam billowed out around her.

"Come on in," she said, holding an arm out for him to take. He refused it and stepped into the hut on his own. She shut the door behind them.

Inside there was only the light from a small iron potbelly stove in the corner, the front door of the stove open to reveal a warm cherry glow. Already he could feel himself beginning to sweat. The back wall was man-length and spotted a knee-height bench, deep enough to stretch out on in comfort. It was lined with fresh-cut cedar boughs, giving off a fine natural aroma.

Atop the stove, steam rose from the rocks in the large metal pan over which Sigrid ladled water. Slocum didn't know whether to run outside and roll in the snow or lie right down and enjoy the odd sensation he was feeling.

"You like it?"

He looked at her through the steam. "I guess so. Feels kind of good, but . . . it's awful hot, Sigrid."

She laughed, a sound he was very much beginning to enjoy. He wished it were lighter in there so he could get a good look at her face. For such a pretty woman, it would be nice to see her face light up when she smiled.

"That is the entire point, John." Then she began unbuttoning her shirt.

"What are you doing?"

She paused. "Well, I am going to take off my clothes and hang them outside. And you are, too. Otherwise they will be wet from the steam."

"But I'm—"

"Put away your little boy thoughts, John Slocum. We are here to sauna."

And before he could protest further, she had slipped out of her clothes and had them draped over her arm. Even in the half-light from the stove, he could see she was all woman, well muscled but soft in all the right places, too. He tried not to stare, and wondered just what he should do about this increasingly odd situation when she made a disgusted sighing sound. She tossed her bundle of clothes onto the boughs and began unbuttoning his shirt.

"Here now, Sigrid . . ."

But she didn't stop. "John, I have seen everything there is to see of you since rolling that grizzly off you. Don't think you are going to surprise me at this time."

"Oh," he said weakly.

"Hurry. We are wasting precious sauna time. I will be back in a moment."

She left, with her clothes, and he heard her bare feet padding down the long dock. Presently a scraping sound reached him. By the time she came back, he was down to his longhandles.

"Those, too." She held out a hand and beckoned for them. He sighed and peeled them off as well. It took him longer than he was used to, because his wounds kept him moving at an old man's pace. He had to admit, though, that the steam felt damn good. Already he was feeling more limber and clear of head than he had in many long days.

He handed her the longhandles and she scooped up the rest of his clothes, then hung them outdoors, with his boots beneath on the steps.

She came back in and doused the rocks with water again. The effect was immediate—he pulled in a deep breath as if urged by the steam. It seemed to fill his entire body with a deep, scorching feeling. Not entirely unpleasant, just damn hot.

"Now what do we do?" he said, wiping the sweat from his brow. Didn't matter, it built right up again, ran down his cheeks and nose.

Again she laughed. "We sit and—"

"Sweat," he said, trying to sound excited about it.

"Yes, exactly. Soon it will feel just right."

And so they sat, side by side, on the soft boughs. She got up after a few minutes and tossed in another chunk of firewood, doused the rocks with water. The steam pulled Slocum's breath from his lungs once again.

He was about to cry uncle when he noticed he did feel better, different, but better somehow. All over, sort of like the feeling he'd get after a long day of setting posts or tracking a deer. A sense of wholeness, of satisfaction. He turned to find her seated beside him again, staring at him.

"You like it?

"I will admit I do like it, yes." He leaned back, allowing himself for the first time since they got there to fully relax. He leaned against the wall and closed his eyes.

"I can tell you like it just fine," she said, giggling.

He opened his eyes and through the steam saw her looking down at his belly. Not really at that, though. And he saw what she was looking at—he was fully aroused and making a fine showing of it.

"That's not what one would expect from such steam," she said, not quite taking her eyes from him there.

"Well, I told you . . . you insisted."

She said nothing, so he blundered on. "You're . . . a beautiful woman. I can't help it. No man could."

"I am glad to hear that. Now just relax."

He did, leaning back once again and closing his eyes. He supposed he should show more gentlemanly decorum, as he'd heard such manners once described, but he figured if she didn't mind, why should he?

He barely flinched when he felt her hands on his legs, on either side of him, gently but firmly massaging his knees, then up his thighs, his waist—her hands kept traveling up his body. He didn't open his eyes, but sat relaxed beyond any feeling he had ever known. All the way up, slowly as she traveled, she was working his body in a skillful massage that served only to deepen his feeling of deep relaxation. He wasn't asleep, just calm in a way he'd not known in a long time, if ever.

Her hands massaged his upper arms, gently along his wounds, just barely touching him there, but her fingertips dancing along his slick skin nonetheless. He raised his hands and rested them on her waist—he knew it would be there, without even looking.

Soon he felt her breath on his face, squinted his eyes open to see her luscious mouth an inch from his, her eyelids closed. And what's more, despite the heat of the room, he felt an even more intense heat at the head of his member. And then that heat wrapped itself around him, and as it descended on him, he knew he was deep inside her.

Sigrid's breath came out in a gentle rush, smelling of mint and sweat, and her lips barely grazed his, their sweat droplets touching, mingling. Her parted lips rested on his above, and she pulled gently on his bottom lip with her mouth, her breath clouding his senses. She held his shoulder and elbow and guided him down until he was flat on his back on the boughs and she above him, straddling him.

She sat up on him, careful not to hurt him, as if she were trying to touch him without touching him. She moved up and down on him as slowly as any woman ever had, and the effect, given that he was so full and throbbing and ready, was as a glass of water to a parched wanderer in the desert.

He opened his eyes and saw her sweat-shining body arched above him, her strong hands resting on the tops of her bent legs. Her breasts, large and firm, swayed, her nipples like ripe raspberries. He reached up to them, mashed them, and squeezed them with his hands. She moaned almost in silence, her moans coming out as sighs, as breezes at the tail end of a workday in late summer when nothing more is expected of you and you're enjoying a tall, cool drink of water.

Soon, though, he tried to speed up the motion. But she was having none of it and kept on with her steady, measured pace. The only thing giving away that she'd understood his intention was a slow smile at the corners of her mouth. And he was glad she'd kept him in check, because it seemed to last twenty minutes or more, and every second of it was pure heavenly delight. He felt as if he were floating.

The end came when the steam began to dissipate and the air grew slightly cooler, though it was still as hot as an oven in the little hut. She sped up, barely, and with a powerful grip that had nothing to do with her hands, he felt them both reach a peak of enjoyment together that was entirely her doing.

If this is what injury means, he thought, I'll take such a recovery every single time I find myself at the far end of a scrape.

She leaned down to his face, kissed his lips lightly, then slowly stepped off him, lifting free, and walking directly to the door. She swung it wide, letting in a blast of raw, cold air. And then she ran. He heard her feet pound along the short dock, heard her offer up a sound between a scream and a shout—and then he heard more screams.

Oh my God, he thought, doing his best to sit upright and instinctively reaching for a Colt, which was not there. He struggled to the door, stronger than he had been when they began the sauna, but still not in top shape.

He heard her shouting, whooping, and laughing as she

pulled herself up the ladder to stand before him, bright red skinned and smiling, her naked body glistening. She had piled up snow on the top of the pond at the base of the ladder, and had jumped into the snow pile. That's what the scraping sound had been.

"I thought you'd hurt yourself," he said, chest pounding and standing at the door of the sauna.

She shook her head and said, "Your turn, John. Hurry, before your skin loses its urge to remain relaxed."

He wanted to say no, but seeing her looking so happy and radiant—he'd not seen her smile so widely and fully—he found himself nodding in agreement. He strode to the end of the dock.

"Use the ladder. Lie in the snow and pull it onto yourself, roll around in it."

He nodded and, still feeling pretty limber from the sauna, gently descended the ladder's few steps to the pond's surface. Without giving himself time to think about it, he collapsed into the snow pile, feeling as though it would stop his heart at any second. He forced himself to roll in it—he kept thinking of how good he was sure to feel. This was something she had just done, after all, and he was tired of feeling doted on and not able to do anything. He would do this, dammit.

But it was almost impossible. Almost. And then he found just his head above the snow. His entire body pounded and throbbed and it felt as though he were burning and freezing in the snow pile, all at once. It was agony and ecstasy, and his lungs screamed.

He forced himself up the ladder, and before he knew it, he was standing on the dock. Sigrid was wrapped in one of the large pieces of flannel, had one held open for him, too. He walked into it and felt instant relief as it wrapped around him. And despite himself, he was smiling. "Whoo!" he shouted. This was something he could get used to.

She smiled, said nothing, but clutching the flannel tight, she made sure everything in the shack was arranged so that the fire would go out of its own accord. Then she pulled on her own boots, tucked her clothes under her arm, and waited for him to do the same. They walked back to the house, the river noise slowly fading behind them.

She walked ahead of him, but was looking down at the path. He saw she still wore a smile. He was glad—so did he. Maybe he would stay awhile longer and heal up fully before deciding what to do. Surely she could use his help with something. But he knew he was wrong about that. She was the most independent woman he'd ever met, and other than what they'd just done, he doubted very much she needed anyone else in her life.

From ahead, her voice broke his reverie. "There is a storm coming," she said softly.

"How can you tell?"

"Can't you smell it? It's in the air, all around us." She smiled at him over her shoulder, the flannel sliding down to reveal just enough of her neck under her pinned-up hair and her bare, freckled shoulder. God, but she was beautiful, he thought. And then he saw movement over her shoulder, beyond the house.

He grabbed her arm. "Hold up there, Sigrid." He nodded. "You've got company."

In the middle of the clearing before the house, a dozen Indian warriors stood fanned in a semicircle. They wore furs, blankets, and snowshoes. Some carried lances, the others cradled rifles. Decorative feathers wagged and danced in the light breeze.

14

"You never said if the Indians are troublesome to you."

"You are correct, I never said." She smiled at him. "But they are not."

She amazed him. She didn't seem afraid in the least, and merely looked at them, sizing up the situation. Just like I would, thought Slocum.

They all stood like that a few moments more, the Indians watching Slocum and Sigrid, and Slocum and Sigrid doing the same to them. Slocum hated the fact that not only was he damn-near naked, he was also unarmed. That was a rare occurrence and not one he liked to think about, should things get ugly. He tried to recall everything old Whiskey Pete had told him about this band of Indians. And it wasn't much.

"Let's take advantage of this lull to get to the house. If they sense weakness in us, it's possible they'll strike."

She actually smiled at him. "Do you think they will attack us?"

"Yeah, it's possible."

Slocum took the lead, edging past Sigrid. She seemed to bristle slightly at this, but he didn't care. He felt that familiar and addictive old tingling at the base of his skull—maybe it was a residual effect of the roll in the snow. He used it as a way to move himself forward, to ignore the pain in his shoulder and leg.

He set his jaw and kept an eye on the warriors, who moved only their eyes. They watched him as he watched them, all the way to the front door of the house. What in hell could they want?

Sigrid was right behind him, but when they got into the front room, he had to close the door behind her. She didn't act frightened in the least. What a strange woman.

"What is your relationship with this band of Cree anyway?" he said as he pulled on his clothes—slower than he would have liked—and rummaged for his guns. "Where are my Colts? My knife? My rifle and cartridges?"

"All there," she said, pulling on a long skirt and nodding toward a stack of familiar-looking goods on a chair near his bed. "But there's no need for violence."

"You know that for certain?" he said, peering out the window. So far the Indians had stayed put.

"I am reasonably certain, yes, that they won't bother us."

"Wish I was," he said, struggling with his boots. Before he could stop her, Sigrid had opened the front door and walked right out, no gun in hand, nothing to protect herself. She had donned her skirt, but only had the flannel covering her top half.

"What are you doing?" he shouted after her. It was then that he saw a larger, older-looking Indian, who had stood in the center of the bunch, walk forward. He carried a rifle cradled in his arms.

Sigrid walked to the end of her path. The man strode up to her, then smiled at her and put his hands on her shoulders and nodded solemnly. He stood back and spoke. When he stopped, he nodded now and again, telling Slocum that Sigrid was now speaking. This went on for a few minutes. Occasionally the old man would look toward the house and nod in Slocum's direction. Then he repeated his smile, gripped her shoulders once more, and turned back to his fellow warriors.

Even as he watched Sigrid come toward the house, the band of warriors backed away. They seemed to disappear in the long expanse of snow and trees, almost as if a stiff breeze had blown them away. Sigrid came back into the house, closed the door behind her. She stood leaning against it, her usual smile replaced with a look of deep concern.

"Is everything all right, Sigrid?"

She looked at him, as if seeing him for the first time. "Oh, yes. I mean, not really, no. They have need of me. The chief's daughter will soon have a baby. And there are the usual winter ills and complaints."

"How did you come to know them? You could have told me they were your friends."

"You did not ask. You merely assumed that because they are Indians, they are my enemies."

Slocum nodded and felt a little foolish standing there with one boot on and his gun belt draped over his shoulder. But what she said next interested him mightily and he forgot all about his momentary embarrassment.

She dropped the flannel and rummaged in drawers built into the wall beside her curtained sleeping alcove, then pulled out a fresh shirt. "The chief also asked if I knew of a golden-haired white man in fancy clothes."

She looked at Slocum. "He said the man had come among them more than a week ago needing help. They pretended with him that they didn't understand English very well, but from what he told me"—she pulled on the shirt, then a sweater over the top, all the while talking to him—"he said he was being chased by a devil man. The chief wondered if that was you." She looked at Slocum, that smile on her face again. "Are you a devil man, John Slocum?"

"Only if you are the Devil Woman of the Rockies, Sigrid." He tried to keep his tone light, but the news of the blond stranger could only mean one thing—it was Delbert Calkins, and he might well be within reach. "What did you tell the chief?"

"That you are definitely not a devil. That the man must be a little crazy in the head."

"How did he take it?"

"I don't think he likes the man very much, nor does he trust him. But it is their way to help strangers, and so he cannot turn him away."

"I hope they don't tell the gold-haired fella they saw me."

"Why is that, John?"

Now it was his turn to be cagey. He didn't want to mix her up in this any more than he had to. So far Delbert didn't seem to know who she was or where she was located. He'd do his best to keep it that way for as long as he was able. "So you were about to tell me more about the Indians, how you came to know them."

"I was? How funny, I don't remember thinking anything like that." She smiled. "But since you asked so politely . . . Many years ago when we first moved here, my father saved the chief's life. Ever since then they have treated me with respect, have protected me, given me gifts. In turn, I help them in whatever ways I can—medicinally mostly. They have come to regard me as a healer of sorts."

"You do have a way about you with such things," he said with a genuine smile on his face. He worked his grizzly-chewed shoulder in a circle, up and down, amazed that it hurt as little as it did. "Yes, ma'am, you really know your stuff. How did you come to acquire such knowledge? No, don't tell me—your father."

"Are you mocking me, John Slocum?"

"No, ma'am. But I am curious about your old man. How did he come to be here? I wanted to ask earlier, but I felt as though I'd be prying."

She smiled. "And now?"

"And now I'm just plain curious. This house, this whole spread, you . . . it all seems so unlikely way up here in the Canadian Rockies."

Her face grew serious as she began selecting various

bottles and crocks from the shelves that lined the kitchen walls. She stayed quiet for a long time and he assumed his probing was not welcome and would go unanswered. She was busy preparing for her journey to the Indian village.

The afternoon's light waned and cold settled in. Slocum built up a fire in the fireplace. Then he spread one of his shirts on the table and began cleaning his pistols.

Finally, as she put a pot of stew on an iron arm that swiveled over the fire, she said, "I am here for the same reasons anyone else comes up here from the States." She went back to the kitchen, then looked at him, a blue clay pot in her hand. "To escape the war."

"Which war would that be?"

"Why, the big war between the North and the South, of course."

Slocum paused in disassembling his pistol and looked at her. "The War Between the States? Sigrid, that's been over for years."

She smiled, shook her head. "Now you are mocking me. I don't believe you."

"Well, I should know, I fought in it. Lost my family, my home . . ." He looked toward the fireplace. "And a few other things, too." Like my freedom to go where I please without worrying I'll be arrested, he thought. It was a fairly direct result of the war that he was now a wanted man.

She said nothing, and grew silent as she continued to sort her herbs and other medicinal ingredients. He figured he'd let that news sink in for a while. Could it be possible that she really hadn't heard that the war, at least as far as governments were concerned, was over? It seemed impossible, laughable even. And yet, she seemed as serious as they come about this.

And she did live her life in extreme isolation. How much company from the States would she have had over the years? Even Whiskey Pete had been afraid of her. Such stories, however they got started, would surely keep others away, at least for a while.

They sat in silence once again, each attending to their own

tasks. Soon the stew on the fire began a slow bubble and the aroma was heavenly. She set two places at the table and ladled out the piping hot meal. She sat across from him, and began to talk again.

"My father was a professor at a college in old New England, just where does not matter now. But when he learned that his school was funded in part with money gained from the slave trade, he had to protest. And then when the issue of slavery was raised, and the rights of all men were being discussed, he was at first heartened. But then the positive discussions turned to talk of war. And killing for any reason other than defending oneself or meat was something my father could not tolerate. He was raising me alone, my mother having died of a fever when I was but a year old."

"He sounds like a brave man, to protest the war like he did."

"Yes, he was brave. He was also practical, and he knew that if such a war began, it would never end." She looked at him sternly. "This he believed and I see little reason to doubt him."

Slocum said nothing, merely nodded, hoping she would continue. He also tasted the hot stew and it was every bit as good as it smelled.

"So Papa packed up our things, and we moved here, many years ago. He wanted to get away—as far away as possible—from the killing and madness of war. He was convinced that it would escalate to such a degree that men would all but kill each other out of existence."

Slocum couldn't help coughing as he spooned in more stew.

"I know what you are thinking," she said, "But he was convinced to such a degree that he did what he thought best and moved here with me, to protect me from the world gone mad, as he put it. It took many months, and then we only made it to the base of the mountains, far down from here. There we stayed for months, and right through one winter. It was cold, but we had built a good winter shelter. We had prepared for the winter there. But it was not far enough for Papa. We were visited twice that winter by trappers, and once by a foul fat man who wanted to buy me from Papa. Can you imagine?"

Slocum thought of the poor woman who'd tried to steal his horse. "Yes, sadly, I can imagine such a thing."

"It took many months and many trips into the mountains, but Papa found this place."

"He selected it well. From what I can tell, you don't get too many visitors."

"Only those who are dumb enough to wake up sleeping grizzlies."

"That reminds me, what did you do with that bear?"

She lifted a spoonful of stew, blew on it. "We are eating him. And I will do so for many months to come."

Slocum raised his eyebrows. "This is the best-tasting bear I've ever had. And his hide?"

"I will give it to the tribe. I leave in the morning."

"You mean 'we' leave."

She frowned. "No, John, you are still too weak for such a trip."

"But you said so yourself that the chief mentioned that a gold-haired man had come among them a few weeks ago. Might be he's still there."

"Why?"

"That man is the reason I came up here in the first place."

"But why is chasing him so important? Can he have done anything that was really that bad?"

"He killed a man, possibly more. And stole a lot of money. Why he headed up this way, I have no idea."

"Perhaps he was just trying to be left alone, trying to get away from you."

"Maybe, but he could have picked a more hospitable terrain." Slocum looked at her, and quickly said, "Not that I have minded some of the experiences I've had here."

"You are kind to say so, but would it not be better to just let him go? It seems that you have already put much fear into him for him to travel this far."

He leaned back in his chair and rubbed a hand over his face.

He was suddenly very tired after such an active day. "I will admit I have given thought to leaving off the chase. But I gave my word to the family he wronged. And my word is something I don't give lightly, nor go back on lightly."

She looked sad, but she nodded her head. "Then we will leave in the morning. You will need you snowshoes, and we can take turns with the sled."

"The sled?" he said. "You mean with the dogs?"

"Yes, of course. Where we are going, the snow is deeper at times, there is much less wind to blow it away, and so it piles deep. It should only take us a day to get there."

Slocum thought about this for a time. "I'll go as far as the Indian village, to see if he's there."

"And if he is not?"

"I'll cross that bridge when I come to it."

She rose and began clearing the table. "What if he is there? What then?"

He pushed his chair back and carried their cups to the dry sink. "I expect I'll get the better of him, hog-tie him, and drag him back to the nearest law enforcement I can find."

"And what if he won't go peaceably?"

"That's a whole lot of what-ifs, Sigrid. As I said earlier, I'll cross those bridges when I get to them."

"Can you promise me that you'll use violence only as a last resort?"

He looked at her looking at him, dirty dishes in her hand, her long hair loose about her shoulders, the dying glow from the fireplace lighting one side of her perfect face. He felt sure he would promise her anything. "That I can do, Sigrid. The last thing I want is bloodshed."

"I believe you, John."

"You never saw the man pass by?"

"No, the trail you were on is only used in warmer weather and by very few people. There just isn't much reason for people to go into the mountains here. There are passes to the south and very far to the north. This way only gets people lost on foot far into the mountains."

"Which is why your father chose it."

"Yes, I suppose so. My home is quite far from that trail, upstream from it and deeper into the mountains."

"Hidden."

"Yes," she said. "I doubt you would have known it was here had I not found you."

He moved closer to her and in a quiet voice said, "I'm mighty glad you did, Sigrid."

Her eyes half closed and she smiled as if just waking up. "So am I." She opened her eyes and looked up at him. "But we must get a good night's sleep if we are to leave early in the morning." She smiled at him. "I believe you know where it is you sleep."

"Yes," he said, not a little confused. But she soon quelled that by saying, "And I will be in my alcove. Good night, John."

"Good night, Sigrid."

It didn't take Slocum long to succumb to sleep, but just before he did, images of lots of deep snow came to him. In his head he heard the growls and roars of the grizzly once again, almost as if they were happening afresh. Over it all he heard a man's laughter echoing long and loud down a valley at him, then everything went white—and he slept.

Slocum woke before dawn to hear Sigrid already up and packing, from the sounds of her bustling in the front room. He lay still a moment, then stretched each limb, working out whatever kinks might have settled in during the night.

He had to get up and cracking, lest she think she was going to sneak off without him. He couldn't let that happen. And he also didn't want to slow her down on her trip to the Cree's winter camp. It was going to be a long day of travel, and truth be told, though he didn't want to admit it to her, he could have used another day or two of rest.

As he began to move around, he felt much better than he figured he had a right to. He wasn't half as stiff or crampy as he thought he'd be. Even his bear-mauled shoulder and leg were not so tender as they had been the morning before. That sauna had some kind of healing properties.

"Good morning," he said to her, emerging from his curtained sleeping nook. "What can I do to get things rolling?"

"You really are set on going with me, aren't you, John?" She smirked at him.

Even perturbed, she couldn't quite frown, couldn't quite lose that edge of smile.

"You bet I am. I came this far, and came through enough hell—and got free of the last batch of it, thanks to you—that I have to go on, have to see it through to some kind of end. Now, any chance I can get a cup of coffee, lady?" He winked at her.

15

Slocum tried to help Sigrid rig up the dogsled and team, but it looked like a tangle of harnesses and yipping dogs to him. He'd give them credit, though, they were a keen bunch, acting like pups who lived for nothing but dragging a sled through the snow. And judging from the smile on her face, Sigrid felt much the same.

Slocum ducked inside the barn, double-checked that the Appaloosa and the packhorse were both well stocked with hay and plenty of feed. And since they could go in and out of the barn at will, there was plenty of room for them to exercise and eat snow when the water in their trough froze, since he wouldn't be there to knock a hole in it.

He hoped the Indians who had visited hadn't gone back and told Delbert Calkins that a strange white man had been at their healer friend's house. That would surely tip off the man and he might well run. But where in the hell would he go?

Cross that bridge when you come to it, Slocum told himself. The man might not be there anyway. And if that's the case, then what?

"All set, John." Sigrid appeared in the doorway. "I am sure the horses will be fine for a couple of days."

"Good, then let's make tracks," he said.

Despite her request that he ride in the sled, Slocum would have none of it. He figured that his strength was at its fullest this early in the day, so why would he relax and let someone else—namely a pack of dogs—drag him around? He felt good and needed the exercise. He started off slow and steady, and it soon became apparent to him that Sigrid was holding the dogs back on his behalf. But he guessed he wasn't loping much slower than a man who hadn't recently been mauled by a grizzly. So in that respect he didn't feel too bad about it.

He was thankful that the initial excitement of the dogs quickly blunted into a steady rhythm for them also. Just as with anything else in life, he mused, slow and steady takes the day. It was impressive to see the dogs lunge through drifts with no fear. They skirted the half-frozen river and for a long while Slocum forgot about whatever lingering aches and pains he might have.

He took in the awesome serenity of the land surrounding him, the valley through which they broke trail. He admired the bold, cliff-like peaks that rose before him. He pulled in deep draughts of icy air that felt good and clean and cleared his head and kept him moving forward.

At Sigrid's insistence, he'd smeared a dark thick grease under each eye, as she had done. It smelled of camphor, pine, pitch, and axle grease. But that, coupled with the low-tugged brim of his hat, did a darn good job at keeping the sun's glare off the snow from blinding him. He wondered how the dogs fared so well, not having any visible means of cutting down the glare. Maybe they kept their eyes squinted enough that it didn't bother them.

An old-time dogsledder had once told him that a dog's sense of smell was equal to that of ten thousand men. It hardly seemed possible, but then again, Slocum figured that since he didn't really know much about dogs, who was he to argue the fact? Another thing to ask Sigrid when they stopped for a breather.

By midday, they had ascended the ridge that separated the

northern end of the terrain that eventually became Sigrid's valley. By cutting long switchbacks into the steep face, Sigrid was able to keep the dogs moving upward. Slocum still kept pace, albeit behind by a few hundred yards, but they weren't getting any farther away from him, and for that he was thankful. His lungs ached with the frigid air that but a few hours before he'd been praising. Now all he wanted was a warm fire, a glass of whiskey, and maybe a nice cigar.

He glanced down briefly to check the strapping on his shoes. The left one felt as though it had come loose, but it looked as if it would hold awhile longer. He guessed she'd stop when the rise leveled off near the top of the long ridge separating this valley from the Indians' winter grounds. He looked forward to reaching it and taking in the views.

As he glanced back up, he saw Sigrid and her team slicing upward fifty yards from the peak, along a particularly narrow shelf. But they were moving along as they should, full of speed and confidence. Sigrid's voice floated to him—her shouts in her native tongue sounded musical and made him want to pick up the pace, too. She was not riding along the tail end of the runners as she did from time to time, but kept a firm grip with her big fur mittens on the long curved handles of the sled.

He admired her tall form beneath her thick wool mackinaw, her head topped with that immense fur cap she'd made for herself. But his smile dropped when he saw one of the dogs in the lead falter. He heard Sigrid's shouts take on a hard urgency. The dog scrambled to get back in line, but it was too late. It pulled the other dogs askew and Slocum instinctively picked up his pace, hoping to reach them.

Then it all went wrong. The dogs tumbled in a welter of ropes and hair, yowling in confusion and pain. He heard their shouts, saw the snow kick up. Sigrid was doing her best to keep the sled angled behind them, if only to prevent it from tipping, but they were headed downslope fast, the dogs' scrambling was for naught, and gravity won.

Slocum cut straight along the slope, hoping to intercept

them before they were dragged too far downslope. Then Sigrid lost control of the sled and Slocum heard a cracking sound like a far-off gunshot, saw the sled roll onto its right side, taking Sigrid with it. Her fur hat flew off, pinwheeled away, and the sled kept going, rolling side over side, gaining speed with each second.

Slocum kicked up a flurry of snow in his zeal to get to them. He stumbled once, righted himself, and lunged at them again. Soon, though, the mad tangle of sled and dogs and Sigrid was a tumbling whir that outdistanced him. From the look of things, her left arm stayed with the sled, even when the entire affair whipped over. Must be caught in the sled's handle, he thought, but he kept on lunging down the slope toward them, bellowing "Sigrid! Sigrid!" until his mouth ached and his lungs and throat were raw.

To his immense relief, they all came to a flailing stop hundreds of yards downslope below him. He raced on, spending half the time sliding on his backside, stumbling down the slope, scraping himself raw on jags of upthrust rock and scree where the snow had been knocked free by the sled's hellish descent.

There was immediate movement from the dogs. Some of them were lodged under the half-broken sled. "Sigrid! Sigrid!" Slocum shouted as he slid the last twenty feet down to them, chanting her name, urging her to wake up.

He reached for her shoulder, dreading that he might find she'd broken her neck, this strong, bold woman. She moaned— a good sign.

"Sigrid?"

"Oh, oh . . . my dogs!" she gasped, and it was then that Slocum saw her left arm was twisted in an awkward way.

The dogs, in answer to her voice, set up a yammering and crying. It sounded both pitiful and excited. For the first time he saw genuine fear and sadness on this strong woman's face. "John," she said, pushing herself to a sitting position. "John, go to my dogs, help them. Cut them free—they won't go far."

"Okay, but don't you move. That arm might be broken."

He held a mittened hand out as if to stop a charging bull. "I'm serious," he said, his breath finally feeling as if it was coming back to him. "Don't move."

"Yes, yes. My dogs, John!"

Slocum crawled around behind her, and made his way to the downhill side of the wreck, which seemed as if it was wedged well, probably against a rock, since nothing moved.

He was glad he had his mittens, because a wounded dog, beloved by her or no, might be inclined to bite him. Despite this, he had to peel one mitten off, tugged it free from his hand with his teeth, and found his knife. While he was at it, he checked his gun belt, but both Colts were still there, strapped tight. Despite his better judgment, he left the mitten off his hand and reached with his other hand to free the dogs. He saw four heads of the six, all eyes on him, all making low yammering sounds. Then one more emerged from under the sled, a determined look on its white-and-black face, its eyes filled with snow. It blinked to see, but with every move it gave a loud, sharp cry.

Behind him he heard Sigrid speaking, but he blocked her out. This was no time for sentiment. He had to get these dogs free in case the sled shifted. Then he had to get Sigrid free. Should have cut free that tangled coat sleeve first, if that's what it had been.

"Sigrid, try to free your arm from the sled, but don't move the sled and don't hurt yourself further. If you can't, then leave it. I'll be there in a minute."

He succeeded in fishing for the nose of the sled, even his mittened hand going numb, and he was thankful that most of the dogs were a few feet away and busy gnawing on their traces, trying to free themselves. Smart animals, he thought, always amazed at the capacity animals had for survival. Smarter than people most of the time, he thought.

There it was, the front of the sled, and there, the leather and rope traces. He cut them close to the rings holding them to the sled, so they would have plenty of free line to work with when they hooked them back up.

"John, have you seen all six dogs? Are they all right?"

"Just five so far, Sigrid." He didn't want to sugarcoat it. He knew there had to be another dog under the sled, but he hadn't heard a thing from it. Before he could move the sled, though, he had to get the other dogs and Sigrid away from it, just in case the sled broke free and continued tumbling down the craggy mountainside.

With a little urging, the half-trapped dog was able to lurch free. The sled creaked, shifted once, then settled. The five freed dogs seemed to sense they were unattached to the sled and moved off in a haphazard, stumbling group a few yards away, diagonally upslope. But as Sigrid had said, they stayed close by. They all appeared none too worse for wear, but he'd have to check their limbs later.

"John, I . . . I don't see Arne . . ."

"That's his name? Arne?" He peered under the sled, brushed away snow, and saw a dog's face, still, glazed eyes, tongue sagged out between teeth, blood on the mottled pink and black nose. Arne . . . dead.

Slocum exhaled a plume of pent-up breath into the frosty air.

"John?"

He said nothing yet, but made his way slowly back to her on his knees, wedging his snowshoes into the slope, praying the sled held on long enough to cut her arm free of the sled handle.

"John . . . is Arne dead?"

He nodded. "I'm sorry, yes. I think it was instant, if that helps."

She stared at the slope, not really focused on anything. Finally she said, "Thank you, John."

He was already working on freeing her arm. It was as he suspected—her coat cuff had become trapped, wrapped around the protruding wood handle, though it probably only twisted like that when the sled began its roll. He looked at her. No tears.

"Sigrid? I need you to focus here. I have to free your arm without jostling the sled."

As he spoke, the sled began to slip. Without the weight of the dogs securing the nose of the battered craft, it had become loosened.

"Sigrid, unbutton your coat . . . now! I thought I had more time, but I was wrong. Get out of the coat, slip your arm out. I have to get above this thing and hold it in place before it heads downslope again and pulls you with it. You might not be so lucky the next time."

He had already made it upslope, and jamming his feet into the slope, with the backs of the snowshoes crossed beneath him, he grabbed the undercarriage of the still heavily laden sled. Its ample load had shifted but remained trussed beneath the canvas tarpaulin and layers of rope.

He'd helped her secure it that morning and knew it was well tied. He took the tip of his left mitten in his hand and pulled it off for a better grip, then with a groan he took on the weight of the sled. The sudden bulk of the load tugged on him while needles of fire raced through his injured left shoulder.

"How's that coat coming?"

"Nearly there," she said, and he could see by the determined look on her face, on her set, muscled jaw, that she knew the gravity of the situation.

One second, two seconds more . . . then the load he thought was well tied shifted downward and pulled him with it. He slid several inches, gritted his teeth, fighting back the urge to shout at her, at anything that might make this situation solve itself. But he knew, as he always did in such moments, that he had to rely on himself alone. Just like you did with the grizzly, Slocum? Stop that nonsense, he told himself. Hold tight to that sled or she'll break her arm, or worse . . .

He watched as Sigrid did her best to tug the injured hand out of the tightly wound sleeve. She had already lost the mitten on the way down, and what he could see of the hand was bluish purple, though he suspected that resulted from the wrenching it had received more than from the cold. Her hand bunched, the sled shifted, Slocum ground his teeth tighter together, and a hiss escaped his mouth.

Then, with a groan that told him her arm was most definitely in pain, she was free. She cradled her injured wing but a moment, then snatched at the twisted coat, unwinding it from the handle. Instead of pulling it over her shoulder, she tossed it aside, and jammed a boot into it, packing it into the snow so it wouldn't slide downhill. She skittered to her right and sat beneath the sled, wedging her boots firmly into the snow downslope.

"What are you doing, Sigrid?" Slocum puffed as he fought to get a better grip on the sled.

"I can hold it better from here. You must unload it, jam the goods into the snow, stack it successively upslope, and it won't go far."

"You should get out of the way. This thing weighs too much; it could roll right over you if it cuts loose."

"Only if it's still packed. You should unload it now before the danger increases, don't you think, John?"

There was that almost playful tone to her voice. But he knew better. She was just telling him that she had made up her mind and he had better do as she said. Besides, he knew she was right. "I'm going to ease off the pressure now. You'll feel it in your shoulder. If the thing starts to cut loose, you promise me you'll lay flat and let it go over you. Put your hands over your head."

"I will. Now unload it, please."

He eased off the rest of the pressure, looking at the load even as he pulled out his knife again. This was not going to be simple. The ropes were a network, all interdependent and all crucial, now more than ever, in keeping the load from shifting. Finally he found a likely spot to slice and he cut the first rope. So far, so good. He cut a second, no movement. Then a third, and the sled leaned toward the back. He grabbed for it. "Sigrid!"

"I'm okay. Hurry, though. Get the weight off it and it will be okay."

He lifted the back edge of the tarpaulin and snaked a hand under. The first thing he found was the bundle of green grizzly hide. She had rolled it in sheeting, then wrapped that, too, in its own canvas, before tying it. Removing its significant weight lessened the load substantially.

The next items came out much easier, and before long he had most of the sled emptied, the various boxes and bundles jammed securely into the slope. He glanced a few times at the dogs, but they all seemed too disturbed by what had happened to come any closer to the sled. To them the thing must represent danger and death.

"I have the sled now, Sigrid. You can get out of there. Put your coat on, I can hear your teeth rattling from up here."

She didn't argue with him, and he could tell by the slowness of her actions that she was cold and hurting. He'd have to get this battered sled to the top, get a fire built—if he could find a sheltered spot—and get her warm. Maybe the dogs would come around by then.

As he worked, he told her what he planned to do and made sure she responded to him.

"I know what you are doing, John, but I am fine. Just cold and sad. I will help you haul these things to the top."

"I understand you want to help, but please, Sigrid, I need you to sit still until I come back. I don't want to risk you trying to climb only to find you feel light-headed. Taking another tumble just won't do, you hear me?"

"John, I cannot leave Arne."

"We won't leave him. I'll get the rest up there, then come back for him. Okay?"

"Yes, okay."

Slocum nodded, though she was looking away again. He pulled in a deep breath and began the long, hard work of dragging the broken sled to the top of the ridge.

16

Nearly two hours later found them partway down the other side of the ridge. He had been relieved to find this side was significantly more treed, boulders more abundant, and the terrain less steep. He could see why she had been in a hurry to get there.

"Thank you, John, for bringing Arne to me." Sigrid nodded toward the canvas-wrapped bundle by her side.

Slocum nodded, but said nothing as he stared into the fire. What a day.

"The others will come closer in time. They are frightened. I still don't know what happened, but I am glad you were here. I don't know what I would have done."

"Yes you do," he said, offering her a half smile. "You would have come through it all just fine and you'd be here by the fire."

"Maybe, maybe not. But I would be alone and without my Arne." She laid her head on his shoulder and he lightly stroked her hair with his hand. "I am glad you were here, John."

"So am I, Sigrid."

A few quiet moments passed, then he said, "How's your arm? Did I wrap it too tight?"

She laughed softly. It was a good sound to hear. He'd been afraid her arm was broken, but despite the wrenching it took, it appeared only to be badly bruised, although enough that she needed to keep it still. Per her instructions, he'd smeared it with one of her liniments, then wrapped it and fashioned a sling for her.

"You worry too much. You did just fine, Dr. Slocum."

"Glad to hear it. You say we're not far from the Cree camp?"

"A few more hours. But I think it best that we spend the night here. I don't feel up to traveling anymore today. And this is a good camp you've made. Well out of the wind, and it looks to be a clear, starry night."

They sat in silence awhile longer. Occasionally a dog whimpered. So far they hadn't wanted Sigrid to tend to them, let alone Slocum. They stayed huddled together, pack-like, just beyond the fire's glow. Slocum watched them, felt sorry for them—Sigrid had said Arne was one of the older dogs, and the father to a couple of the others.

"They will be fine," Sigrid said, as if reading his mind. "They only need some time to think about what has happened."

"Maybe they feel guilty?"

Sigrid had laughed at this, but then nodded. "It is possible. Dogs feel much more than people give them credit for. But guilt? I am not sure about that. Perhaps."

"Sigrid, what can you tell me about the tribe?"

She drew a deep breath, let it out slowly. "Let me see. They are a band of Cree, but long ago they split from the main tribe. There was an argument about leadership, if I remember correctly what my father told me. This took place so long ago that some of the younger members no longer know the real reason for the split. You would call them a rogue band, but they consider themselves content. They prefer to live alone, isolated in their little mountain valley."

Slocum nodded. "I can understand why. Even with all this snow and cold, it's a beautiful place to be."

"Mmm," she said. "Now it's my turn to ask a question."

"Okay, let me have it."

"This man you are chasing. You said he killed a man. What if he isn't there with the tribe?"

"Aha, you are asking a question you already asked me last night." He smiled. "Seems to me I said I'd cross that bridge when I got to it."

"And that hasn't changed?"

"I guess not. As I said, I will admit I have toyed with the idea of calling it quits, but that doesn't sit well with me, makes me feel lazy. And I don't like the idea of tasting that in the back of my throat for the rest of my days."

She nodded. "Yes, I can understand that." She yawned and closed her eyes. "You will do what you need to do, John Slocum, and I know you will make the right choice when you do."

Early the next morning, Slocum awoke to see Sigrid sitting across from him, on the other side of the fire, in the midst of her dogs. They were all leaned against her, as if they each had to touch her somehow. She was smiling and stroking their ears and necks.

"Good morning, John," she said.

"And to you." He nodded, stood, and stretched. He was stiff after that big day of rough work and not being in top condition to begin with. "Well, I better get the sled attended to, see what sort of repairs I can give it, at least enough to get us to the village."

Together, they inspected the damaged sled and found that one runner had snapped, but was still in place, and the entire framework had been stressed and suffered cracks along several pieces. But in the new day's light, it looked more serviceable than he had imagined it would. "I bet we can have this pup mended in no time." He rubbed his hands together and said, "Tell you what. I'll get started on this if I can coerce you into making a pot of coffee . . ." Slocum looked at her hopefully.

"That sounds like a fair trade. Coffee it is then."

*   *   *

The Cree village, which Slocum chose to think of it as, since he wasn't sure how else to consider the breakaway band, was not what he'd expected. They had built log and sod huts dug into the hillside. He counted at least twenty of them, and they all faced down along a wide span of valley cut through with a river that must have been even prettier in summer.

The mountains loomed up large almost on three sides of them, but somehow the spot, though much higher up in the mountains than Sigrid's place, seemed comfortable and homey, not barren and isolated as he'd pictured it.

The huts faced a number of what he assumed were communal fixtures such as a large fire pit, and pole racks for drying game. Off to the side stood what looked like a stone and mortar dome, man height and with an arched tiny doorway halfway up. "What is that?" said Slocum, nodding toward it.

"That is an oven for baking bread and smoking meats and other foods. My father helped them build it."

"Smart man, that father of yours."

She touched his sleeve. "John, they are good people, but they are wary of whites. Not many strangers have been through these parts. Please let me introduce you. It would be better that way."

"Sure—I'd feel the same way." He paused and gestured before him. "Ladies first."

As soon as they were within sight of the little village, children came running out the entrances of the huts, mothers chasing after them, shouting.

"Kids are the same anywhere," said Slocum quietly.

The dogs pulled the mended sled and reconfigured load fairly well, considering their obvious aches and pains and the sled's cobbled condition. Slocum looked over at Sigrid and she was smiling. These people, he saw now, were as close to family as she had. He realized he knew very little at all about this amazing woman or her life here. Who would have guessed that such people lived—and thrived—in so isolated a place?

It seemed the entire tribe emptied out of the huts and drew

tightly around Sigrid, talking and gently touching her, asking questions and kneeling to stroke the dogs. Their looks of concern for her and the dogs emphasized to him the level of their friendship with her.

Slocum had intentionally kept off to the side. He busied himself with looking at everything he could, searching for any sign of Delbert Calkins, while removing his snowshoes and fiddling with the harnesses. If Calkins had been the one they'd mentioned, and he must have been—how many blond dandies were roaming the Canadian Rockies?—then Slocum wanted to end this here and now. Finally Sigrid turned to him, smiling. She beckoned for him to come over. He did, smiling and nodding at them.

The younger men, some of whom he seemed to recognize from two days before, all regarded him with serious gazes, almost like brothers scrutinizing a potential suitor for their sister, while the older men bore the distinct hard stares of fathers and grandfathers. They all had folded arms. But the women smiled at him, and the children, obviously fully trusting of Sigrid, swarmed around him, giggling and laughing and clutching his legs.

Sigrid said something and they all laughed. Even the men cracked smiles.

Slocum smiled, too, and said, "What did you say?"

"That you didn't know you were so popular with children, but that it seems you are willing to learn—whether you want to or not."

He nodded. "Did you explain your arm, and other things?"

"Yes," she said.

"Please ask them about Delbert Calkins."

"Who?"

"The golden-haired man with the fancy clothes. If he's here, I need to know before he makes a run for it."

She did as he asked and the adults' faces grew grim again. "What did they say, Sigrid?"

"That he was here, but . . ." She looked at the faces of her friends again, as if unsure about what they said.

"Sigrid, not telling me won't make it go away."

She turned back to him. "If I tell you, John, then you will leave."

"That bad?"

She said nothing, but slowly nodded. "He left, but only this morning. Chief Mis-it Ha says he will help you to find him if capturing the man means that much to you. It is up to you, John. There is a very good chance that the man you seek will not make it over the mountains. The tribe did outfit him with a better coat and mittens, but only because he came to them so ill equipped and nearly dead. His horse died on the trail not far from here when he tried to force it through deep snows. But when the men returned from seeking me, they happened to tell him that there was another white man close by, someone they had not ever seen before. That is when he began acting strange."

Slocum watched the men's faces as she spoke, and it was obvious from their slight nods that some of them understood what she was saying.

"This morning they noticed he was gone and so was a pair of snowshoes." She looked at him gravely. "John, they want to know why you seek him, what he could have done to deserve to have a lawman from the States follow him all this way, to terrify him so that he would risk his life in the high rocks."

Slocum breathed deeply and nodded. "Sigrid, please tell them the truth. That he is a murderer of at least one person. He ruined a family, broke a young girl's heart, and stole a whole lot of money from a whole lot of people. And make sure they know that I am not a lawman."

"Then what are you?" It was the chief who spoke and to hear him speak such plain English startled Slocum. He had expected that some of them would comprehend much of what he said, but to hear such a response was a surprise.

"I am a man who agreed to help the family retrieve their money and, most importantly, to see that the man who killed the young man—he was a son and a brother—is brought back to the United States city where he committed the crime. There he will be dealt with in a court of law."

The entire time Slocum spoke, he watched the chief's face, but it was impassive. The two men seemed instead to engage in a second conversation at the same time, one with their eyes, each sizing up the other, each measuring the other against his own definition of a man.

"I will help you," said the chief. "I do not want this man near us. Now that I know what he has done, I see now why I did not like him. He has done bad things and he came to us wearing too much of a false smile. He was too kind, too much of everything to be a good man who had lost his way. I was suspicious of him and I was right to be."

Sigrid cleared her throat. "Mis-it Ha, if you will pardon me for saying so, do you think it wise to go on such a dangerous journey when your daughter is about to give birth?"

The chief smiled, touched Sigrid's shoulder. "Daughter of Lars, that is why I must go. My daughter's husband cannot go. He has too much to live for and I have lived a full life. If I do not come back, then it will be as it should be."

Slocum shook his head. "I appreciate your kind offer, Chief, but I have tracked the man this far alone and I can follow through to the end just fine."

"The way you did with the grizzly, John?"

For the first time, Slocum saw genuine anger on Sigrid's face. Before he could respond, she turned away and, parting through the crowd, began untying the loaded sled. Soon she was offered assistance by women and children, who also untied the dogs. The entire mass of chattering people headed toward one of the dugouts, where he assumed they'd find the pregnant girl, the chief's daughter.

Slocum turned back to the men, a dozen of whom stood before him, with the same puzzled, curious looks on their faces as before.

"What did she mean when she spoke of the grizzly?" said the chief.

The other men, too, gleaned enough of the question that

they leaned forward, curious to hear his tale. Slocum nodded and said, "Okay then, might as well tell the entire embarrassing tale."

And he did. They all nodded at the appropriate times, raised their eyebrows in understated surprise when they heard of what Slocum had been sure would be his final memories on earth—the effort of trying to end the bear's assault by stabbing at it with his Bowie knife.

"And you did end up killing the bear with your knife? That is . . . very good work." The chief was obviously impressed, and spoke to the men beside him. They nodded back to him and then to Slocum.

He hated to disappoint them, but he had to do it. "No." He shook his head. "It was Sigrid." He nodded toward the hut she had disappeared into. "With a Sharps rifle. She shot it and it collapsed on me. The next thing I knew I woke up in her house, all bandaged and tended to by her."

The chief spoke briefly to his men, gesturing toward Slocum and thrusting his chin toward the hut. They spoke low among themselves for a few moments. Then the chief turned once again to him. "You are a lucky man, John Slocum, to have found such a gift as the daughter of Lars."

"I know I am. More than you can imagine. She is an amazing woman."

"Then you also know what she means to us all."

"I have a pretty good idea of it, yes."

"Good, then I don't think I need to say more about that. We will protect her with our lives, you see. And that is why I must go with you."

Slocum's confusion must have been apparent on his face, because the chief said, "There is only one way that man can come. And it is down out of the mountains. He cannot get over the mountains the way he thinks. We are able to take care of him here, now that we know what sort of a man he is. We will not offer him any more of our kindness. But there are other ways he could take to come down from where he went."

The chief's eyes rose, and Slocum and a few of the other

men looked west, toward what looked like a pass in the high peaks. As if to emphasize the danger of what they were looking at, a cold wind sliced at them from the north and made them all hunch under their furs. Slocum bunched the collar of his sheepskin coat tight with a mittened hand.

"If the man comes down the only other way I believe he can, that would bring him down into the valley of the daughter of Lars. And then she would be in danger. This cannot happen."

"I understand. I do not want that any more than you do. But what makes you think he won't be able to make it through that pass up there?"

The chief smiled as if he were looking at a simple child. "That pass is not a pass. Just below where we are now looking is a steep cliff face. The rocks are impossible to climb. And it is rimmed with much snow high up. It is not a good place to be even in the warm time."

"And in the winter?" said Slocum.

"In the winter, as you call it, that place can be impossible to leave."

Slocum said nothing, but thought much about what the chief had said. He followed the men to the central fire pit and warmed his hands, eventually taking off his mittens, grateful for the heat.

Finally the chief spoke. "She is angry with you, but you know that."

Slocum nodded, kept staring at the flames.

"It is because she thinks much of you, John Slocum."

"And I her. But if that man has cornered himself, I need to get to him before he dies up there. If he figures out a way to come down that other passage you mentioned, the only other way down—and that seems most likely as he knows that this way would only lead him back to you here, people he stole from, then that means he would find his way to Sigrid's. And that, as you say, cannot happen."

Barely an hour later found Slocum slipping over his shoulders the straps of a woven pack basket in which he'd transferred a few essential items from his gear. A small, wizened Indian woman had given him a bundle of dried elk and bear meat, for which he was grateful. It smelled quite good and he'd no doubt it would serve him well in the harsh reaches ahead.

He double-checked his knife, his pistols, his ammunition, and lastly, his snowshoes. They were secured tightly to his boots. How long he could wear them he didn't know, but if Delbert Calkins had worn a similar pair into the mountain pass, then so could he.

Lastly, he slung over his shoulder a borrowed sheath for his rifle. He was afraid the fur-wrapped sling might slide off his sheepskin coat, so he slipped it across his chest, bandolier style. It would be more difficult to grab in that position, but he doubted Delbert was anywhere nearby—at least not for a while yet.

He asked the chief that should anything happen to him, and if Sigrid was delayed at the village, could he please send someone to her place to tend to his horses. The chief had immediately handed the task to one of the young men, who nodded gravely at Slocum. That made him feel better about the coming trip. One last thing he didn't have to worry about.

"The daughter of Lars will understand that you do this for good reason, John Slocum."

He turned to face the chief, who was similarly outfitted, though clad in even more fur-trimmed hide garments than he'd worn earlier. The man seemed to be a good many years older than Slocum, but there was a toughness about him that belied his age.

Nonetheless, Slocum wished he were going at this alone. He'd tried his best to dissuade the man from accompanying him. He'd made the case that this was his fight, that ultimately he was the one responsible for driving the thieving killer into their midst, but the old man would hear none of it.

When Slocum turned to the other men of the small band of Cree, in hopes of gaining some look of support from one of them, they all looked away. So instead of pushing it further and risk angering these obviously proud people, he had smiled and agreed with a nod of his head.

And now they were ready to depart, but still Sigrid had not come out to see them off. Slocum's concern for her, and his guilt over the situation, must have shown on his face. And he was sure the old man was pretty good at reading people's faces.

"You seem sure about that." Slocum smiled, but the old man looked surprised.

"I have known the daughter of Lars for a long time. She understands more than you know. We must leave now if we are to make the first peak before dark."

"Don't you have to say good-bye to anyone?"

"Why would I do that?" said the chief, again with a surprised look on his face. "To do such a thing would be to admit the possibility of defeat. And that is not acceptable."

And to Slocum's surprise, the old man cracked a smile. He was starting to like this chief. "Then let's head on out," said Slocum.

They made it fifty feet up a low trail winding behind the huts when Slocum heard his name shouted from below. He stopped, just behind the chief, who also paused and looked back.

"I told you—the daughter of Lars." He nodded toward Sigrid, striding up the trail toward them, her arm still in the sling.

"Sigrid, I—"

"I came to give you this." She handed him a small jar of the ointment she'd been rubbing into his shoulder and leg wounds. "You will need it." Her jaw was set hard, her eyes glinted.

"That all?" he heard himself say, harsher than he'd intended, but her frosty demeanor rankled him.

"No. You must take care of yourself, John Slocum. If the man you seek is as you say, then he is hardly worth risking your good life for."

He could only nod. She smiled at him then, and turned back to the village. He watched her for a few moments, wishing he were staying with her, wishing he had hugged her, wishing he had at least said thank you to her, the woman who had saved his life.

The chief tapped his shoulder and they turned and resumed their climb. In a moment, the chief said, without turning, "The daughter of Lars—"

"I know, I know," said Slocum. "She understands more than I know."

He could have sworn he heard the chief chuckle.

17

Whoever that son of a bitch was, thought Delbert Calkins, he wasn't giving up on him—that much became pretty clear once those damn Indians had come back from wherever it was they went the other day. He'd been stuck in the camp with all those women and children, and one or two young men and a couple of old ones. They all seemed to trust him, but he noticed they didn't let him go anywhere alone but to attend to his personal necessities.

A white man they'd never seen before, they said. Then they'd looked at him almost as if they were accusing him of something. And he supposed they had been. All because he made the mistake of telling them when he first stumbled into their camp that he was chased by a white devil man. He had hoped that would invoke a bit of charity and fear in them, and at the time it had worked pretty well, he had to say.

They took him in, gave him food, warmer clothes, told him he could stay until spring. Though of that, he had no intention. As soon as he could, he was headed for that mountain pass high above the Indians' valley. They said it was not possible to get through there, but what did they know? They were a little ragged tribe of Indians living in the mountains in winter. They didn't even have sense enough to get on out of there come snowfall. Shoot, he bet once he got on the other side of those mountains, he'd be looking at green grass and birds and trees and the lush valleys of California. He had to be close to California by now . . .

So when he heard that they'd invited some crazy healer woman to the camp to help with that pregnant Injun about ready to pop, and they said she was the same one harboring the new white stranger, he knew it was now or never. He had to make a break for that pass.

The night before he had waited until they were all asleep. Slipping out would prove no problem because they stuck him in a little hut with a fat snoring Indian who farted all night. It was like being stuck in a den with a bear. Yet another reason why civilized men should dwell in cities and not in this godawful place he had gotten himself lost in.

He had bundled himself up in the fur coat and hat and mittens they had given him, checked his pistols and money, and had stolen some of the dried meat they all seemed to eat—had Indians not heard of proper food? Soon enough he'd found himself outside, paused after clunking shut the low, heavy door of the dugout—the fat one slept on, snoring and farting.

Delbert had smiled to himself then, excited to finally be on his way. A day or two at most and he knew he'd be through that pass and into the promised land. He would lie naked in the sun for a whole day, stretched out on green grass once he got up and over the mountains. But first he had to get there. His eyes fell on a pair of snowshoes leaned against the little hut. Fine—they were built for the fat one, but they would get him up and over the mountains. He grabbed them and headed up the trail.

The moon was half-size and served on this crisp, starry night to light his way sufficiently enough. Every few minutes, Delbert patted his torso, where inside the coat resided his money, the most valuable thing he had. He would have need of it in California.

The going was easier than he'd expected, and the trail ran

alongside the burbling, half-frozen brook that flowed through the Indians' valley below, widening into more significance as it rolled along. Before long, the trail ended at the source of the brook. There looked to be much tramped and packed snow by a pool the Indians had obviously carved out.

Much of the pool, some twenty feet in diameter, had frozen over, but the constant rush of water out of the rock wall kept it flowing from its source down into the pool.

He regarded the cold, ever-running water. It made him thirsty, so he drank. Then the flowing water made him feel as if he had to urinate. A sudden smile played on his face and he yanked off his mittens and worked loose the buttons on his trousers. It took a few moments, but the sound of the running water did the trick. Soon he let loose with a steaming stream—straight into the spot at the edge of the pool that it was obvious the Indians had chipped open to retrieve drinking water.

"Damn Injuns," he said, shaking his head as he buttoned up. He giggled once again and strapped on the snowshoes. "Serves 'em right for ending the path here. Now I have to make my own way over the pass. So be it."

And soon he was swinging his arms in counterrhythm to his legs' strides, deeper into the rising jags of rifts and peaks, higher and higher toward that beautiful, tempting, promising pass.

18

Slocum followed the chief along a well-used trail packed into the snow. It roughly paralleled the brook the entire way up. He figured they'd come to the source of it before long, and sure enough, a few minutes later they reached a pool—and the end of the trail.

The chief paused beside it, staring. Slocum was grateful for the brief rest it would offer, and for the chance of a cool drink.

"I guess this is where your people get their water."

The chief didn't respond. Slocum followed his sightline down to a drizzled line of yellow snow that ended at the edge of the pool, where a spot had been chipped and cleared.

The chief finally looked at Slocum. "Would he think so little of us to do such a thing?"

"I'm afraid so, Chief. I tried to explain the sort of man he is."

"This is no man we are after," said the chief, adjusting the straps on his pack. "This is a diseased dog. Now, let us drink . . . upstream from his leavings. Then we will be on our way before the storm comes."

"Storm?"

"Yes, John Slocum. Do you not smell it on the wind?"

Slocum closed his eyes and breathed deeply. There was that familiar bite to the air, but with something to it that reminded him of the taste of metal. "Yes, now that you mention it, I can."

After they'd drunk their fill from the frigid burbling water, they continued onward, easily following the snowshoe trail Delbert Calkins had left behind.

What must the chief be thinking? wondered Slocum as he fell into a steady rhythm behind the chief.

The going grew more difficult the farther into the mountains they climbed. The air chilled, the breeze ceased altogether, and they felt the first faint touches of snow drops on their faces. The calm before the storm. Slocum knew the wind would soon pick up and the snow would really begin to lash at them.

Each man knew that the other wanted to push on until they had no choice, no way to move forward without misstepping, for the snow would wipe away most if not all traces of Delbert's tracks. From what the chief had told him, there were few options for their quarry anyway. No trails out but the one they were now following. They had already passed the spot where he might descend down out of the passes toward Sigrid's valley, and saw no sign of his tracks there. That meant he was still ahead of them.

Still, despite what the chief had said, Slocum did wonder if there wasn't some way through the pass, some route the Cree hadn't found. They had seemed just a pinch superstitious about it when he'd mentioned tracking Calkins up here.

"I can't imagine he'll be much more than dead when we find him, Chief. In fact, I'm mighty surprised he's lasted this long."

The older man paused, half turned, and eyed Slocum. Both men breathed deeply, their breath pluming into the chill air.

"But there is a reason he has lasted this long, John Slocum. He has something that not many men have. But you have it. I think I have it, too. Do you know what I speak of?"

"Maybe, but tell me just the same."

"The man you seek has a fighting heart. He will not be defeated—even when he finally is defeated, he will not admit it, will not believe it is happening to him. And so, he will never truly die. He will never become a satisfied spirit."

"Is that what I'm destined for, then?" Slocum watched the thickening snowflakes settle, then melt on the man's weathered cheeks, his long nose.

"Perhaps." He shrugged. "I do not know, John Slocum. I am only a man." He began walking again. "But I do know that you should not think so little of this man you seek. He may be a bad one, a diseased dog, but he is a smart one. He will not like being cornered."

Slocum nodded, even though the old man was staring ahead, working his way up the steepening trail. The chief had given him food for thought and maybe a warning, too. Maybe he was underestimating Delbert Calkins. After all, the chief and his people had spent a whole lot more time with Calkins than Slocum ever had. Hell, any time they spent with the murdering bastard was more time than Slocum had.

Still, thought Slocum, I'd like to come up on his near-frozen body. That would make my life a whole lot easier. An angry frozen man, I can deal with. Drag him back to civilization, thaw him out, and let the judges and juries and lawyers do the rest.

After another hour, the chief paused, held out his arm in front of him. Neither man could see the end of his mitten. "We will stop here. I believe I know the spot, and it is wide enough that we will not tumble away to the bottom in our sleep."

That shocked Slocum, as he'd been under the impression that they were still surrounded on both sides by the steep rock walls they'd been climbing between in a narrow, winding crevice. But now that he looked down, he saw, with the help of an errant wind gust, that they'd been trudging along close by the trail's edge. It dropped off to his right, though how far down he didn't know. Nor did he want to.

"Come," said the old man, tugging Slocum's sleeve. He

led him to the left, to where the trail widened into an alcove, one edge of which was formed such that it blocked the full brunt of the snowfall and gusting winds.

As they settled back against the crusted wall, Slocum was surprised that the chief suggested they make a small fire.

"It is safe—and I am not as young as you are. I am like an old woman sometimes. The cold gets into my bones and mocks me. I would like to drive it out of my fingers, at least."

In short order, they had a meager fire built with a small collection of tinder and twigs the chief produced from his basket. It was just enough to warm their hands and faces— and that was just enough to raise smiles on their faces.

"Have any of your people been up here recently?" Slocum said, chewing a piece of dried bear.

The old man chewed his own hunk of meat thoughtfully, swallowed, then said, "If you are asking how I know there is no pass ahead, it is because I have been as far as it is able to go there. And I am still on this side of the mountains. So that should tell you something." He smiled.

"That pretty much tells me all I need to know, yes." Slocum grinned and chewed another piece of meat.

After another lengthy pause, the chief said, "There is one thing you should know about it. The place is filled with bad medicine that is trapped there—falling snows and circles of wind. It is a place where no life can survive. The bad things cannot leave. Once you enter there, it is very difficult to get away. Always it pulls at you to come back. But you would be wise to stay away . . . if you are lucky enough to get away in the first place."

"Like you," said Slocum.

The old man nodded. "Yes, but . . ." He raised his hands as if testing the air for rain. "Look at where I am—I have come back here now. But that, too, is as it should be."

That was the last thing either of them said for the night. Each man leaned back against the rock wall, bundled in their coats and filled with their thoughts, as their meager fired guttered and died out.

As Slocum drifted into a deep sleep, despite the cold, his thoughts mutated from bright, sunlit things to shadowed, gloomy entities that stretched and wavered like long, ancient shadows soaking upward into canyon walls until they covered everything with a thick gloom. And over it all like a hawk's shrill cry echoed mocking laughter.

19

Delbert Calkins awoke in a dark, cold place, his jaw stiff from the cold, too stiff to allow his teeth to chatter, though he knew they wanted to. He lay still for a few minutes, trying to recall just where he was—ah yes, being chased by that determined fool—and just what he'd done to lead himself here.

It all came back to him slowly, as if viewed under murky water. The girl, sure that's where this had begun. He wasn't troubled by killing the girl's annoying brother, even though he knew they expected him to be. But such things had never bothered him. He figured he was part of the great animal kingdom, as one of his old schoolteachers at Saint Ursuline had once called everything that was alive but wasn't a plant or a man.

Why was it all right for animals to kill one another to take something they needed from the other, but not people? He had asked the question in the schoolroom, so long ago but he remembered it like it had happened just the day before. But the only answer he'd received was a clout to the head that set his ear ringing for weeks and got him sent to the headmaster's office for a caning.

And that hurt nearly as long as the ear did. But the thing that hurt the worst had been the other students—even the ones he thought were his friends. They hadn't laughed when he'd asked the question. In fact, he knew that some of them wondered the same thing. But they had laughed when he had been clouted by that pinch-faced Brother Barnabas.

Why was it fine and dandy for the teacher to clout him and the headmaster to cane him, but not for him to strike back? He lay there in the snow, rubbing a hand along the side of his head, still feeling the smarting sting all those years later.

Then he remembered where he was and smiled. He'd proven them wrong so many times over the years. People are nothing more than part of the great animal kingdom. If someone has something I want or need, just like a lion or a bear or an eagle, I will take it. And if they fight me, I will injure them. And if they keep on fighting me, I will kill them. This I have done and this I will continue to do. It is survival of the fittest.

This was something he guessed that the man who had chased him all this way knew only too well. It was a shame they were engaged in this foolish chase, because in different circumstances, they might become chummy. Certainly they could share such thoughts, for they were both obviously of the same mind. One man pitted against another. There could only be one way this would end—Delbert would kill the fool chasing him, of course.

He grunted to a sitting position, snow falling off his arms and chest. He blew it away from his whiskers and mustache and pulled a mitten off. He tried to twist and curl the ends of his mustache but they were having none of it—the wax and oil had long since vanished. When I get to Frisco, I will luxuriate in the finest hotel for a week. I will be bathed by Chinese girls and anointed in oils from the Orient. And I will make damn sure I shave.

And if my money should run out, I will find more and then take it. With the thought of his money, his heart thudded faster and his bare hand patted his coat and found no familiar bump!

But it had to be—it was there the night before when he fell asleep—and then he did feel it. His coat had shifted in the night, just enough to cause him needless worry.

"Get up, Delbert," he said out loud to the still, cold morning. "Today is the day you cross the mountains to the promised land. To a warm place with food and liquor and gambling halls and pretty young things eager for all the fun in the world."

He stood, brushed the caked granular snow from his clothes, stomped the life back into his ice-cold legs, and looked upward. It had been dark the night before by the time he had made it to the narrowed end of the steep canyon. Too dark to risk venturing into what he assumed was a continuation—albeit a narrowed one—of the pass. Why risk taking the wrong route because of darkness when you are so close to freedom?

But now he stood, shivering and looking upward, at the point where the steep blue-gray rock walls towered over him, pinched to a near-close, like the bow of a ship a hundred feet before him. They were impossibly tall, and the only things breaking up the seemingly endless edifice of blue-gray rock were clumps of snow that had stuck in the driving storm of the day before.

Everywhere he saw sharp angles filled with nothing but black shadows. Sunlight must have been lighting it, and yet the overall vision was one of dark and eternal near-dark. He forced himself to look all the way up to where the massive rock walls ended. Rafts of gray-tinged snow daggered through with great tentacles of ice, overhung the sides like frozen ocean waves. They were the sort of things that only come in dreams, the sort of dreams no one ever wants.

Great reefs of snow and ice overhung the rock, so high up it hurt his neck to see them. And beyond them, far above, he saw a sky the flat color of gun steel.

Delbert Calkins groaned and ran up the talus slope covered in loose snow, falling to his knees as he dug in. He tried to climb it, tried to prove to himself what he knew could not be—that there was a passage at that dark place where the rock walls met. He lunged again and again at the slope, sliding backward, dislodging snow and making the lower edge of the slope into a greasy mess. His breath hurt, shot out in bursts, and he finally flopped to the ground, panting.

Then he gazed at the big cumbersome snowshoes and his mouth tightened in anger. He tore at their bindings and finally managed to rip them from his boots. He threw them away from him and, seething, made another lunging dash at the slope. He made it higher than he had before, but then could go no higher and slid backward again on his hands and knees.

He sat at the bottom, throwing snow and rock from him, bellowing his rage at the dark, stone walls. Far away, he heard thunder and did not care. He sat still for long minutes, then when his anger ceased to tremble him and his teeth stopped grinding against one another, he sat still and regarded the object of his intentions far above—the narrowed gap.

There had to be a way through—he just had to get up there. Sure it would be tight, but anything worth having was worth working for, right, Delbert? he told himself. And he stood up with a new idea in mind.

20

"Chief . . ." Slocum nudged the old man. It was early but they needed to get up and moving. He slowly unbent himself and even more slowly stood.

He was as sore as he could remember being since the grizzly mauling, but he had no time or desire to pull off his coat and slather on Sigrid's tincture. Too damn cold, even if he had the urge to do such a thing. Plenty of time for that later. Once he was back on the trail, he'd be fine, limbered up and stretching. He looked down at the old sleeping man. What little of the man's face he could see looked a lot older than he had the day before when he'd seemed so spry. But now he just looked old.

"Chief?" He bent low and nudged the man's shoulder again. The man didn't move.

Slocum tugged off his mittens and dropped to his knees. "No, no, don't do this to me, Chief. Come on . . ."

But beneath his fur wrap, the old Cree warrior's cheeks were stiff and cold, no breath puffed from his blue lips. A look of stony contentment decorated his face. Slocum slowly let out his own breath. "Dammit," he said softly. He covered the man's face once more, and left him as he was, leaned against the rock wall, his hands folded in his lap. He could well have been sleeping.

"Well, Chief, you made it back." He looked out across the trail, up toward the mass of gray rock not far ahead. "Or it pulled you back." He looked down at the man. "I'll return for you, though something tells me you might not want to be moved from here. I'll think on it. But first, I have something to do."

He tied on and tightened his snowshoes, unsheathed his rifle, checked his pistols and his knife. Then he headed out, away from the alcove, and up the trail, staying close to the wall.

Soon the trail widened and grew steeper. Far ahead he saw that it widened farther, opening out into an upslope of snow and shale, all gray-white snow and tumble-down jags of raw-edged rock from on high. The closer he drew, the darker and more foreboding it became. The walls seemed to gain dozens of feet with each step he took. And at their tops, where they met, angling westward against the spine of the mountain range, rested great curving rafts of glistening iced snow, like eyebrows topping a massive stone face.

Slocum licked his lips and slowed, but forced himself to keep on walking. No wonder the old man didn't want to come here in the dark. He couldn't imagine waking in the morning to this sight. And then he heard something. He stopped and cocked his head. He plucked off a mitten and lifted the side of his fur cap. There it was again, what sounded like screams, coming from far ahead. Screams of anger, of outright rage.

And Slocum smiled.

21

"I have you now, you bastard." Slocum did little more than mumble it into the scarf wrapped tight around his face. He jacked a shell into play in the rifle and lumbered forward.

Since he awoke, he'd been vaguely aware that the landscape this high up in the rocks had become much the same as it always looked in the high places he'd ever been to. But there was something extra about this place that seemed almost more barren and forlorn than anywhere else he'd ever been.

Slocum didn't really know just what it was that made it so, but the chief's words about the place not letting you go, about calling you back, kept ringing in his head, echoing like a ricochet shot inside his skull.

And now that he heard the shouts of the only creature on earth other than himself to be in this place of desperation, one killer by the name of Delbert Calkins, Slocum felt— despite the fact that he wasn't a particularly spiritual man—as if he'd come to a place of reckoning, a place where two would meet and one would win. But would one be able, or even allowed, to leave?

I aim to find out, he vowed. And he trudged on, his eyes fixed on the gray, shadowed place before him. From this vantage point, he saw that there was no place to go—the great rock walls narrowed to nothing. Unless there was a slim opening that led through the mountain to the other side, this was as the chief and his men had said—a dead end. In more ways than one, mused Slocum.

Another few yards and Slocum saw movement in that grim place far ahead. But it hardly looked like a man's movements—something kept scrambling up, then sliding back down a long slope of scree and jagged rock, hunks of the cliffs above that had sheared off over time.

Didn't look like a man, and yet it had to be Calkins. Slocum was just too far away yet to see whatever it was clearly. He doubled his pace, but crouched, too, as he moved forward. He had no desire to spend the entire day up here—let alone another night. The sooner he dealt with this madman, the better it would be for them all.

He was thankful for the new layer of thick snow that had fallen in the night, because it helped dampen the sliding, clattering sounds his snowshoes made against the crusted surface of the trail. The minutes seemed to tick by slower. The closer he drew, the more distinct the sounds from the creature became. And the creature, it was now obvious, became a man.

All other logical reasons aside, it had to be Delbert Calkins because Slocum wanted it to be him, needed it to be him. Something inside him demanded it. He'd been through too much on this long, sometimes foolish trip, and he'd be damned if he was going to be robbed of this chance now.

Slocum became acutely aware of his breathing, hard and labored and edged with a wheezing from the effort he'd expended so far, efforts that were already depleting his lowered levels of strength and ability. He had never been more aware than now of his injuries from the grizzly. He tried to block out thoughts of the healing wonders of Sigrid and her ointments, massages, and sauna.

Slocum followed the trail along a sharp upturn, around a massive blackish tumbledown boulder. Then the trail switched back sharp to the left, upturned again, and he found himself in easy sight of the man. He was within fifty yards or so, and what Slocum saw amazed him and filled him with rare hope.

So this was Delbert, once and for all. He was blond and had his back turned to Slocum. He also didn't appear to be an overly large man, but of decent build and average height. He was coatless, his outer garments—a fur wrap from the Indians and a wool mackinaw—having been tossed aside in a pile halfway between himself and Slocum.

Calkins stood facing the scree heap, his arms hanging by his sides, his shirt untucked, his arms rising up and down with his heaving chest. He'd obviously been working hard at getting up the pile, and it was just as obvious to Slocum that he'd been unsuccessful, judging by the churned mess of the slope before him.

Slocum kept walking forward, leveling his rifle at the man at the same time. Suddenly the man began shouting at the top of his voice. He bent double, clutched his head with clawing, desperate hands, pulled at his hair, then shook his cold-reddened fists at the defeating slope before him. The entire time he faced the pile, keeping his back to Slocum and the trail.

Slocum used the man's shrieking fit to close the gap between them by half. He ended up just shy of the discarded coat—the sleeves were inside out and mittens and snowshoes lay some yards off in opposite directions, as if ripped off and thrown away in anger and haste. Just before he guessed he'd be heard, Slocum stopped and raised the rifle higher, curled a finger around the trigger.

When he spoke, it was with a hard and sharp voice that cut the air. "Now Delbert . . ."

His sudden words scared his prey into a scream even as he turned to face Slocum.

Slocum continued: "Should you make it to the top of that scree heap—and I'm not saying you will—were you planning on coming back down for your coat? Seems unlikely, but then again, so is everything you've done in the past few weeks."

Delbert Calkins faced him, his face a red, sweaty thing, eyes bulging from rage and exhaustion, his shirt sagged half-open. He seemed to take a long time to figure out just what it was he was facing—a man with a gun. A man who knew his name.

Surely he's aware he's still being followed, thought Slocum. He said so to the Cree.

Then the blond man smiled, a fake grimace that pulled the dropped ends of his mustache wide. One hand rose a few inches as he spoke. "I have been expecting you, though I had hoped you'd be dead or would have grown bored with bothering me."

Slocum saw that the untucked shirt half concealed a holstered pistol. He raised his rifle an inch, wagged the end. "Keep your hands still—in fact, raise them high. I know you can do that, Calkins. I saw you holding your head as if it were about to explode just a few seconds ago."

That seemed to strike a nerve in the angry man. His pasted-on smile dropped away and his eyes burned like black coals at Slocum. He slowly raised his arms to chest height.

"Higher, Delbert. Put some effort into it. Or are you too tired from jousting with that hillside?" Slocum stepped once, twice toward the discarded coat. He kicked it with the edge of a snowshoe. "Aren't you cold, Delbert?"

"Don't touch that!" the man shouted, his lips pulled tight against his teeth. The veins in his neck and on his temple stood out, throbbing.

"Oh?" said Slocum, dragging out the word and doing his best to sound infuriatingly calm. From Calkins's trembling face and clenching hands, it was working. "Hands higher, Delbert. Otherwise I may be forced to shoot you."

Calkins snorted as if he'd heard a lousy joke, shook his head. "She sent you, didn't she?"

"Who might that be, Delbert?"

"That little rich bitch. That foolish brother of hers should have let me be. And her father, what a waste—all that money and he just sits on it. Doesn't like to gamble, he told me. Have you ever heard such a thing? Doesn't approve of it, didn't approve of me. Ha! I showed them."

Slocum said nothing, just stared at Calkins.

The two men quietly regarded each other for a few moments, Delbert's breath not slowing much, as if he were a steam train working hard on an uphill grade.

"There's no way through here, you know," said Slocum finally. "No way at all." The effect was startling and immediate.

"You shut your mouth! There has to be a way out! Has to be! I—"

"You what, Delbert? You want it to be, so therefore it has to be?" Slocum shook his head. Even as he thought it, he knew that not long before, he had wished for this man to be Delbert Calkins and he had been.

Slocum guessed that Sigrid and the chief would agree that wishes could be powerful things, but not when you're faced with a big old rock wall.

"Look," said Calkins in a calmer voice. "I don't know who you are, but you don't have any right to follow me. Why are you bothering me? Why is this any concern of yours?"

Slocum mentally ticked through all the reasons that he knew of—murder, multiple thefts, being downright nasty, using people for nothing more than personal gain, and so many more reasons. But he finally said, "Because you peed in the water supply of the village of my friends."

For a moment, he guessed he'd surprised Delbert Calkins. The man stood wide eyed. Then he laughed, bent double, and slapped his knees, howling. Too late, Slocum saw the reason for these theatrics—Calkins had snatched up the pistol and worked to shuck it from his holster, but his untucked shirttail got in the way. It slowed him down a few beats behind Slocum.

But Slocum knew he couldn't shoot him. Not because the man didn't deserve it, not because he wouldn't be justified in killing him right here and now for drawing on him. But because the chief's words once again came to him. This was a foul place filled with bad medicine. At the same time, Slocum caught quick sight of the massive rafts of snow towering over the gray gloom of the pass that never was a pass.

He ran forward, his snowshoes more of an impediment

than ever, his rifle held out before him, ready to shoot if he had to. "No, Delbert! Don't shoot! You do and we'll both die." He could tell that Calkins was a little surprised that he hadn't shot him, that he'd let him nearly pull his gun free.

"That's the idea, isn't it, bounty hunter?"

Slocum shook his head and spoke urgently in a low voice. "Haven't you ever heard of an avalanche? You pull that trigger and not only will you never make it any closer to the pass you feel for sure exists, but you will never leave this foul place alive. Nor dead either, I'm sure of it." Slocum was sure he got through to the man, but he was equally sure that Calkins was too bullheaded or too far gone to acknowledge the truth of what he was telling him.

The chief had said that the man had an inner fire, that spark that Slocum also had that kept him from giving up on a thing—no matter if reason shouted contradictions in his ear and logic poked him in the nose.

If what he'd said got through to Calkins, Slocum couldn't see it on the man's face. He had to keep him preoccupied, had to keep him from clawing out that pistol the rest of the way. If he knew Slocum wouldn't shoot him because of the danger from above, Calkins was loopy enough that he would shoot Slocum, and to devil with the consequences.

"What makes you think there's a pass through there anyway, Delbert?"

"Stop talking to me like you know me. You don't know me and I don't know you. Hell, I don't even like you." The entire time Calkins spoke he maintained his half-crouched position, poised and ready to pull the pistol free and blast Slocum to hell.

"There sure as hell has to be a way through to the other side, to the promised land of—"

"Of what, Delbert? What's so great about the other side of those mountains anyway?" Despite the wire-tight tension, he was curious to know why Calkins had come up this far in the first place, and why he thought getting over the mountains would solve all his problems.

"You have to be kidding! We're a stone's throw from California—just over that ridge is green, green grass, sunshine, birds, and far down below, where the land levels off, there's the coast, San Francisco maybe. I'll take my money and make more money, then I'll get on a train and head to the Mighty Mississippi and buy me a riverboat and gamble all the time. All the time!"

Calkins shouted out loud now, his voice echoing all around them, spanging off the sheer gray rock and shattering in every direction. "Money and power and fame and women and money and card games and gold and money, money, money! And I'll be as far from these damned mountains as I can get, back in a city where civilized people live, drinking good wine and smoking the best cigars and eating fancy meals served under silver domes . . ."

The madman's last remark reminded him of Ginny Garfield and her room service meals. Concentrate, Slocum, he told himself.

"Delbert, the only thing over that ridge up there"—Slocum jerked his chin skyward without taking his eyes off Calkins—"is more mountains. You are about as far from California as you could hope to be. We are in the Canadian Rockies. Far north of the U.S. border, and even farther north of the Northern California border. You are in a world of snow and ice, kid. Give up this foolishness and come back down with me. We can both get a warm meal by a fire, maybe scare up some whiskey. Just look up, Delbert."

Even though Calkins didn't rise to the bait, Slocum was sure Calkins knew what was up there—and what it could do. All that snow up there perched like a big curl, like an outthrust lip of defiance, hanging hundreds of feet up on all three sides of the dead-end canyon pass.

"You're lying, damn your hide!" Calkins's voice reached a raw, full-throated bellow, spiraling upward into the gray sky, and was answered with a sound like far-off thunder.

Slocum winced involuntarily.

"That scare you, bounty hunter?"

Slocum forced a smile. "Not hardly, kid." But it had, and he didn't like where this entire conversation was going—nowhere and fast.

"Then how about this!" Delbert jerked the pistol free of his holster.

Still, Slocum did not pull the trigger, couldn't risk it.

"What's the matter with you, bounty hunter?" Calkins screamed it at him. "Bring me that coat! Bring it now!"

Slocum shook his head. "No sir. You want it, you come get it." Maybe Slocum could lure Calkins over closer, then jam the rifle into his head, knock him out cold.

Just then the building thunder from high above became louder. "Delbert, don't move," Slocum whispered at him. "Just don't say a thing. Let's get out of here. We can argue later. Come on!"

"That ain't nothing but thunder, you idiot," said Calkins, smiling as though he were looking at a defenseless beef animal about to be slaughtered.

"Thunder?" whispered Slocum. "In the middle of winter? On a mountaintop? You damn fool, it's an avalanche! We need to get out of here!" The entire time he spoke, he backed away from Calkins. "Now shut your mouth and follow me. Otherwise you'll get us killed." But the kid didn't move. Slocum shook his head. "Don't fire that gun, Delbert."

Delbert thought for a moment, then smiled. "To hell with you." He threw his head back, but kept his eyes on Slocum, "You hear me?" he roared. "To hell with you all! There is a way through, bounty hunter. I'll get there, you wait and see!"

Then he cranked back on the hammer.

Slocum had no choice—even as he yelled, *"Nooo,"* he dropped to his left side and rolled, touching off the trigger and hoping like hell he hadn't taken the bullet that sizzled out of Calkins's gun just before his.

22

Sound like nothing Slocum had ever heard before blotted out everything. At the same time, it was more than sound. It was massive and raw and full and it pushed down on him. When he threw himself to his side, he landed on Delbert Calkins's coat. Now he snatched it up even as he struggled to get back to his feet. He jammed the rifle barrel forward, leaned on it, straightening the snowshoes from underneath himself.

He knew he was shouting, but he heard only an incredible whooshing filling his ears. He looked for Delbert but couldn't see a thing but spumes of white. Even the gray cliffs had vanished. His face felt hot and sounds like the hoofbeats of giant horses thundered closer.

Slocum lunged forward, heading down the trail, and for a few seconds he thought he might make it, just might outrun the wall of snow that sounded as big as the whole world.

And then something shoved him square in the back, as if a giant's fist had punched him between the shoulder blades. He felt himself rise off solid ground and whip, end over end, through the air. Something hard slammed against his head but it hardly mattered. If this was the end, he knew there were worse ways to go. But there were better ones, too.

Smothering under so many feet of hard-packed snow wasn't something he looked forward to. Still he kept rolling and tumbling, his knees hitting hardness—the ground?—before he was lifted up again and shoved farther along. One last time his legs slammed against something unyielding and then he was pushed forward, facedown. The world turned instantly from a pure white wall of infinite sounds to a pure black and silent thing.

How long he lay that way, Slocum had no way of knowing. But he heard a voice, a familiar voice, telling him to get up, to not forget his inner spirit, the fire that had kept him alive so many other times. It sounded like the chief. But that would be impossible—the man had died. Hadn't he? Maybe he had only been sleeping, maybe he had faked death so that Slocum had to go on . . . to do what?

And then he remembered—Delbert Calkins. The man had gone crazy right before his eyes, had abandoned all logic and given himself over completely to the foolish notion that he was just a short climb to the sunshine and green meadows of California.

Slocum became aware of needing something, something . . . breath. He was running out of air, had to breathe. He tried but felt only hard pressure on his back, on his front. He was buried in snow. That damned Calkins had shouted and screamed and brought the very heavens down on them both. Slocum remembered running, then not running, but being pushed. It had been the snow, carrying him along. How far had it taken him? How deep was he buried?

Buried! The thought of dying this way knotted his gut deep inside and he fought to push himself upward with his arms, the arms that were jammed beneath him. And inch by inch it worked. He was able to move his hands, then his feet, then his knees, and soon his elbows worked back and forth and his head up and down.

He pushed at the snow with his chin, tried to empty his mouth of the stuff, but still he could not breathe. His body ached for air, his chest felt as though it were flattening, his head ready to collapse. In the last burst of energy and effort he knew he would ever have, he pushed with that damned inner fire and . . . light, bright and blinding, flooded his eyes.

He coughed, gagged, and spat what felt like an entire body full of snow from his mouth, blew it from his nose, and at the same time gulped greedily of the stuff he needed more than anything, felt that if he didn't get it soon, he would exhale for the last time, black out, and never again wake up. His lungs ached and he didn't care.

As long as he pulled in air and pushed it out again, he was alive. He did it again and again, his eyes flooding with tears, his nose and mouth gagging and spitting and breathing.

When he was once again able to focus his vision and breathe without thinking about it, Slocum looked about himself. He didn't recognize much, but he thought he might be facing downslope, along the trail he'd walked up. He didn't really care. The sun on his bare head felt good. His arms were still beneath him; only his head poked out of the snow. He heard his voice then, laughing, a hoarse, gasping sound, and it was one of the best sounds he'd ever heard.

Slowly, slowly he dug himself out, working his hands back and forth, back and forth until they swam to the surface. The snow was loose and granular, and moved easier than if it were melted and hardened into itself. His arms felt unbroken, but sore. He rested that way, his arms stretched out before him as if he were about to dive into a pond. He felt as though he might be standing upright, and had not been facedown as he'd thought before.

He moved his legs in a kicking motion. At least he thought they were moving. It was difficult to know. When he felt he'd gained sufficient wind, he stretched his arms out to the sides and pushed down with them.

It took long minutes, but he eventually felt himself rising upward, inch by inch. As he lifted, the loose snow filled in underneath his boots, giving him something to push against. Soon he was able to work his legs back and forth and help his arms by pushing upward. And then he was free.

With a mighty last effort, he flopped out of the hole—he had been standing upright, though leaning forward slightly. He lay there for long minutes, gasping and moaning and wanting to whoop for joy that he was alive. But he didn't have the damned strength to do much more than breathe. So he contented himself with that fine task. He also noticed that he didn't have his snowshoes—the force of the avalanche must have ripped them right off his boots. He wasn't about to dig for them. The thought made him smile.

He must have dozed off and begun dreaming, because the next thing he knew, he heard voices shouting. Over and over, he heard the voices shouting his name and other words, words he did not know. He raised his head and tried to look around, but everything was so bright he had a hard time seeing anything but sunlight bouncing off snow in every direction all at once.

"John! John Slocum!"

It was a woman's voice and it was close. Dream or not, he figured it couldn't hurt to answer. "Here . . . here I am!" He tried to shout, but it came out ragged and croaky.

"There you are!" and someone was there, beside him, lifting his head, blocking out the bright light. He looked up and into Sigrid's smiling face.

"Sigrid . . . are you okay?"

"Of course, silly man. It is not I who survived an avalanche."

"Help me up."

She did, and he sat leaning against her. Other voices drew close, saying things in a foreign tongue—the Cree, he recognized them now. The chief. He was dead, he must tell them. But wait, he'd heard his voice, hadn't he?

"The chief, Sigrid. He's . . ."

"We know, John. We found him. It was what he wanted. Why he came with you in the first place."

"What?"

"Yes, we all knew it. This place, it was something he talked of often. We thought that since you were so determined to come up here, he should be the one to guide you, even though we all knew we probably would not see him again. And it is so."

Then three Cree warriors came closer, leaned down over him. One of them reached down and tugged on something sticking up from the snow—Slocum's rifle. The three men were smiling and patting him hard on the shoulders and head.

"But . . . the chief. Aren't they bothered that he's dead?"

"No," she smiled. "They are happy for him. It is honorable. It is as he wished it to be. And he has helped you, has he not?"

Slocum pushed away from her, sat up straight. "What? How did you know that?"

Her face grew serious. "Chief Mis-it Ha was a most interesting man. He was my father's best friend, and a good friend to me as well. And a fine leader for his small band of Cree."

She hadn't really answered his question, but Slocum figured that was as it should be. Best not to think about it too much or pick at it, else it might come apart and mean less than it should.

"The man you sought . . . is he . . ."

Slocum nodded. "He tried to beat the mountain, but this was one game he couldn't win."

The mention of Delbert reminded him of the man's coat. It must have held his valuables; perhaps he'd find some of the stolen goods in its pockets. Then just as quickly as the thought occurred to him, it vanished. He would surely have lost his grip on it in the avalanche. Still, he looked down into the slumped snow-filled hole he'd pulled himself out of and saw a ragged edge of cloth. Could it be?

He reached down, grasped it in his hand, and pulled. But it was stuck, jammed under too much snow. The three warriors all lent a hand and pulled the thing free in seconds. They held it up and it was indeed Delbert Calkins's wool mackinaw.

Seeing it made Slocum almost wish he hadn't tracked the man so relentlessly. Calkins might still have died, but at least not goaded on by him. Then again, maybe he would not have gotten so confused and headed so far north into the mountains.

Maybe he would have gone on to some other city and fleeced and murdered his way through a lifetime of Ginny Garfields. Maybe Slocum had done a good thing in pursuing him so hard. He would have to believe that; otherwise he would doubt himself about it for the rest of his days. And if he kept on living like he had the past few weeks, those days would be short ones, indeed.

He turned to Sigrid. "Let's go home."

She smiled at him and helped him to his feet with her one good arm. The five of them tramped down the snowed-in trail.

Before they rounded the last curve that blocked the view of the great gray walls from below, Slocum noticed that the dead-end pass had filled with enough snow that a man could probably climb right up it and over the top. And as he turned back to the trail, he couldn't help laughing.

23

They lay sprawled before the fireplace, exhausted after running the dogs and exercising the horses. It had been another long day out of weeks of long days filled with hard work, but it had been a good day. And with the promise of a sauna later. Darkness had crept up on them, however, so Slocum and Sigrid satisfied themselves with a quick wash and now delicious stew smells filled the air in the cottage.

Each of them was half-clad. He'd long since grown accustomed to seeing Sigrid walk around the place without a shirt, or with a shirt unbuttoned. It was her custom, and since she felt no self-consciousness about it, why should he? Slocum didn't think he needed to do anything more than enjoy seeing the sight of a beautiful woman who was so comfortable being herself she didn't mind if he admired her. And if he guessed right, she seemed to like it, too.

As if in response to his thoughts, she half lay atop him, her breasts squashed against his chest. "John?"

"Yes," he said, opening his eyes.

"I would like to make love right now."

He raised his head and looked at her. It was rare enough thing to hear from a woman that he thought she might be toying with him. But her face, her liquid eyes, and her grasping hands all told him otherwise.

Soon they were gripping each other in a tight embrace, their lips found each other's, and they stayed that way for long minutes. She reached down and he felt her long, strong fingers unbuttoning his denims. The whole time she probed his mouth with her tongue. He gave as good as he got, and reveled in the notion that this woman, no matter how much hard work she underwent that day, would always have time for this . . .

She raised herself up a bit off his chest and he sought her perfect breasts as they hung before his face, luscious, low-hanging fruit ready and ripe for the plucking. He reached for them with his mouth while his hands slid along her hips, slipping off the loosened skirt down beyond the curves of her fulsome backside.

She squirmed, helping him, and he pushed the skirt as far down as far as he could reach, then trailed a hand back up between her thighs, tickling her. He felt the heat from her push against him. He kissed and gently teased her pert nipples, then worked his way up between her breasts, trailing a line with his tongue tip up to her throat, her head thrown back as she ground herself against him.

Soon it became too much for either of them, and in mutual agreement she reached for his long, thick member and teased herself with it for just a moment. Then she raised herself up slightly, and slid down on it, all the way to the bottom.

Sigrid's breath came out in a quiet stutter that ended in a gasp as Slocum teased her breasts, one with a finger and thumb, the other in his mouth. She smiled, but didn't open her eyes. In the dim light from the fire in the grate behind them, her face took on a rainbow of earthy hues. It was as if the sun were setting all over her face, her long wild hair that hung about him, as if he were walking through a dense, hot jungle.

Soon she sped up her motion, at times raising only her hips, at other times working her entire body, each person matching the other's movements with an equal counterrhythm that drove the other to greater heights of pleasure.

A tingle deep within each of them grew more demanding, crowding out all other sensations, tightening until they gripped each other. Their mutual bucking locked them together in a taut, unmoving embrace. They spasmed once, twice, three times, and slowly relaxed into each other.

With Sigrid there was no screaming, no howling as he'd known with other women. Just an intense, quiet whole-body tingle and tremor that seemed to linger nicely for long minutes after they had collapsed in a sweating, heavy-breathed tangle of arms, legs, hair, and lazy kisses. She lay to the side, so that they faced each other, but were still connected in the most intimate way, and each stared at the other, not speaking, but watching the light from the fireplace dance in each other's eyes.

"Shhh, do you hear that?"

Slocum reflexively reached for his pistol, but Sigrid stopped him, and shook her head. "It's no cause for alarm."

"What is it then?" he said, easing back against the rug.

"It is the sound of spring."

He listened and heard it, too, the quiet but steady *drip-drip-drip* of snow melting from the eaves. He smiled, looked at her, but her smile had faded. "What's wrong?"

"That means you will leave soon."

"Well . . ."

"No, John. It is the way it must be. You said so yourself once we got back from . . . that unfortunate occurrence in the mountains above the village."

"I can't say I'm sorry we've been socked in with those blizzards. I can't think of a nicer place to be than here with you."

"You are good to say that, but now you must return to the States. You must ease that girl's mind about the man who murdered her brother."

"Yes. And I have a pretty blue stone I have to give back to a certain old mountain man. I think he'll be tickled to see it again."

She smiled. "You are a good man, John Slocum."

"No, Sigrid. *You* are the good one."

24

Almost two weeks later to the day, greening grass showed in patches throughout the open space before the house. Beyond the trees they heard the mighty rush of the river as spring runoff from the high peaks raced south to the sea.

Slocum was all packed and ready to go. He stood by the Appaloosa, who had put on weight and didn't seem too interested in what he suspected was in store for him—a long journey with a man on his back.

"I'd like for you to keep the packhorse, Sigrid. I have no use for him now and he's a stouthearted little beast. He has good legs under him and he likes snow travel. Not like the Appy here." Slocum gently slapped the big horse's shoulder and the horse nickered, tossed his head. "Besides, that little horse will get you to the village in quick shape should the need arise."

"I appreciate that, John. He and I have become close friends. There is something about that little horse that belongs here somehow."

"I agree."

They were silent for a few moments, then he said, "Is there anything you might like? From the States, I mean?" He knew better than to mention fashions or fancy foods. She didn't seem to want or need such things.

She smiled. "No, John. There is nothing I need. I have my books, my dogs . . ."

"Your sauna . . ."

She nodded, "Yes, I have that, too. I am content."

"You are special, Sigrid. That's for sure. I will miss your company."

"And I you, John Slocum. You may visit me from time to time, if you so wish. You will always be welcome here in my home and in my bed. But I would ask that you please do not tell others about me nor bring others by here. I very much like my privacy. Much like my friends, the Cree."

"I understand, Sigrid. And I'll respect those wishes. Truth be told, if I thought I could be happy in such a place, I'd be tempted to invite myself to stay on for a bit. But—"

Already she was shaking her head no. "As I said, I like my privacy. And you"—she smiled—"you, John Slocum, like other things too much, and that would be bad for me. Too much of something can be . . ."

"Too much?" he said, smiling back at her.

She nodded. "And besides, you also are a wanderer. You have things to do and places to see that you would always be thinking about. Places that are far from here and you need to find them and learn about them. Maybe one day you will be willing to become rooted, but I doubt it will happen anytime soon."

He sighed, put a hand on the saddle horn. "I think you may be one of the wisest people I have ever met."

"No," she said. "Maybe just observant."

"And one of the humblest." He rubbed her arm, squeezed it. "Good-bye, Sigrid. Take care of yourself. You are a wonder." He kissed her on the cheek and mounted up.

"And you, John Slocum. Be good to yourself. There is much to enjoy in the world. Don't let the angry ones change you."

"I'll do my best." He touched his hat brim, looked at her pretty face one last time, and rode southeast, down out of the mountains.